PROMETHEUZ

Book #2 of the XREAL Series

by

Will Lorimer

For you and me

CHAPTER 1

MEAT BOX on Channel KDXP: – *chewin' the
fat* 23.00 -23.-05- **9/9/43.**

'Hey, ah heah Fatberg's gotta beau.'

'Yea, word's goin' round. But,
personally ah don't believe nuthin' 'bout Man
till ah see't 'n black 'n white.'

'Print media's gone, Dude.'

'You know wha' ah mean. Bitch story's
a PR wheeze.'

'Au contraire. Fatberg's flesh and
blood, same as you 'n' ah. Count 'n it. He's
gotta have a squeeze tucked away
sum'wheah.'

'Yea, suah Fatlover.' (laughs) 'Only
entanglin' he'd get down to, is ol' soissant
neuff!' head down 'tween vinyl thighs da late
model Pricilla. Man's coldah th'n a witches' tit,
ah sweah. All he ca-ahs foah is 'massin'
mwoah moola.'

'And that, Dude, is why he's wheah he
be right now.'

'Yea ah heah'd, Fatlover.' (sighs). 'Been depressin' me some. Only one way to go foah de likes. Ain't no mountain high 'nuff foah d' MF, as ol' song say.'

'No valley deep 'nuff.' (sings, basso)

'Now ain't dat de truth.'

'Fatberg dwon't do nuddin' widout weason, Dude.'

'Now dat's sum'thin' we *can* agwee oan, Fatlover. Man's always gotta plan.'

*

Quite some time has elapsed since Jake was cocooned in a mesh of sticky silk strands ejected by one of the City Eye's MRDRs – (unaffectionately known and feared as 'Sky Spiders.) and some time too since he'd been awake.

'Mr Cousins?'

'Who? What?' Prising open his gummy eyelids, Jake's first sensation was of falling towards a dazzling cityscape composed of countless shimmering lines, spreading out below him. But then his world tilted, the lines reformed and he found himself looking up instead of down, and into the wrinkled face of a tall thin man stooping over him.

'Mr Cousins,' the man repeated, in an anglo, nasal accent of mangled vowels and mutilated diphthongs. 'Are you awake yet?'

'Yea, I guess,' Jake said, becoming aware he was tightly gripping an AI helmet, which he dimly recognized to be a Sanyon Mark 3. Setting it down delicately, next to him on the narrow bed, he elbowed himself into a sitting position, then leaned back against the cold metal wall, needing the support. 'Where am I?' he said, a horrible suspicion dawning as his confines swam into focus.

'A-ha,' the tall man chuckled, as if Jake had just said something witty. He was wearing an ill-fitting velvet suit of a lurid shade of green. 'Come now, Mr Cousins,' he said, gesturing a spade hand at the surroundings, 'surely you recognize this?' He smiled lopsidedly. 'After all, *you* designed it.'

'It's not the subs, is it?' Jake croaked, his mouth dry as a desert rat's sphincter and throat rough as grade 3 sandpaper.

'Is that what you call the Subterranean Holding Facility for the Intentionally Homeless?' the man asked, shaking his big head in wry amusement. 'Subs,' he repeated, his rubbery lips peeling back to expose a full set of yellow teeth in his gaunt face, which now reminded Jake of a grinning skull.

The man thrust forth a hand, and as Jake tentatively shook it, said,

'May I say it is an honor to welcome you, Mr Cousins.' He dipped his head. 'My name is George M. George, that's my first name and surname. Never mind the M.' He shrugged. 'My mother and her fancies. Only today – ah, this morning actually,' he chuckled, 'I was *officially* appointed the Director of this wonderful new Facility, ahem.' He coughed behind his hand. 'Whereas previously I was only the ah, *acting* Director.'

'I see. Delighted, I'm sure, and … congratulations too,' Jake mumbled, wondering if he was dreaming, the man's weird manner and posh accent putting him in mind of a ham actor whose name he had forgotten, who played creepy villains in the old British horror movies he'd watched as a child in his bedroom. 'So what happens next, Mr Director … George George, sir?'

'A-ha yes. Presently, we have, er … something of an emergency below, and I, ah, that is, we were … er … hoping you would so kind as to assist us with, um, it.'

'Anything I can do to help.' Jake attempted a smile with his cracked lips. 'But please, first I need to change out of my clothes. I feel like I've been in them for a week.'

'I think you will find it has been rather longer than that, Mr Cousins.'

'Really?'

'Actually, you were in suspended animation for a total of twenty-two days in the cold store at the City Eye.'

'So long?' Jake said, with astonishment. 'No wonder I'm so hungry.'

Turning aside, George George spoke rapidly into his wrist monitor. 'GG here, order Jim in C-level to rustle up something for our newest resident, will you? He needs feeding up.'

Ending the call, he looked down at Jake. 'Unfortunately, the delay at City Eye was unavoidable, Mr Cousins.'

'Why?'

'Because only today, as in only three hours ago, is the Facility at last fit to receive inmates.' George George beamed.

Jake pointed to a neat pile of overalls he had only now noticed on a shelf just to the side. 'I suppose those are for me?'

'Yes, yes, regulation apparel. Pink for inmates, blue for guardians, and green for the, uh, executive branch.' He chuckled throatily, revealing that he was an illicit smoker, an activity which these past three years had been forbidden anywhere in the City by a municipal ordinance, enacted under the Emergency Regulations. 'Which is just me, presently, as yet the facility is only operating at one tenth capacity. But not this old suit,' he added, apologetically, fingering the worn lapel of his green jacket. 'I purchased this for a wedding many moons ago.' He smiled lopsidedly. 'My wedding, actually. I should have heeded the advice of my mother, who said that green was an unlucky colour for the groom, a prediction which all too soon proved correct, I am sorry to say, but I wanted to be different and so chose green. Where was I?' He chuckled again. 'Oh yes, my Executive Director's suit. For that I am still waiting. Ha ha, City Eye didn't have a size in green to fit.'

Despite the thick smog below where he was perched, on the old watertank on the roof of the Pierspoint building, very little escaped the It's penetrating gaze, as he studied the mesh of energy lines that connected everything in the city below with everything else beyond.

Jake.2, as we will come to know him, is the iteration of Jake Cousins. Though this proposition undeniable, the question of who came first is less clear, is less clear. Experts have even argued, the physical body is the creation of the IT.

However this may be, presently, Jake.2 is exploring the material world which for him has only just sprung into existence. Brand new, as the saying goes. Like that iridescent flying thing which Jake would have immediately identified as a Super 8 Predator WatchGog but Jake.2, with his limited knowledge of the world, could not yet name.

Rising out of the smog on its 8 rotors, it veers towards him, but then, after circling above, detecting nothing with its thermal sensors, it flies off, logging the man-shaped haze that first attracted its attention as a swarm of insects above the old water tower on top of the Pierspoint building.

Jake.2 has picked out one line in particular from the myriad of luminous fibers that zip and fizz over the city. Just one line out of incalculable billions, among the layer upon layer of complexities that outline every feature of the city, together with every bump and cranny of its underlying topology – all the way back to when the land was thickly forested and only sparsely populated by hunting and fishing communities along the coast.

Each line connects two points, which could be near as a pair of eyebrows or distant as points in neighboring galaxies. Although, that latter type is surpassing rare, as Jake.2 will discover in his exploration of the world and its blinkered inhabitants, who from an early age learn to categorize and objectify everything in it, and by so doing deny the true nature of their world, which is but one skin of multiple spheres of existence. But for now, his main focus is on – *has to be* on – that thrumming line, which forms one side of a triangular configuration, connecting a woman in the apartment below where he stands to someone on the far side of the planet, who in turn is connected to –

What started out as mutual animosity between Carrie and Julius (who just about everyone else in the world knew only as 'Fatberg') and mutated into uneasy familiarity after Jake was sectioned under the Emergency powers, had developed into something approximating intimacy – albeit, remote. Their burgeoning relationship was necessarily conducted at long distance, as Fatberg flitted between continents, delivering on his promise to shareholders of FakeReal by snapping up high altitude prime real estate in bargain deals from governments that had been bankrupted by the massive state subsidies required to maintain the worldwide shut-in.

'Julius.' Carrie smiled beatifically at her protector, framed in her 3d box monitor, which showed him seated behind his desk, against the backdrop of a large blacked out window. 'So where is it today?'

He held up a hand. 'Before I answer that, first the good news. Your ex is fully conscious again. '

Carrie sighed with relief. 'Do you know anything else?'

'His body stats are absolutely fine, the medics report. I've fixed things with the new man in charge, and we both agree that getting him involved in an ex-officio role which plays to his strengths will be his best cure. The subs are the biggest step yet towards shrinking the human footprint on the planet and there will be plenty to keep him busy down below, with all that's going on there. And, who knows, with his background, and a nod from me, he may end up in charge of the whole program. So now you know there's absolutely no need to worry about him anymore, okay?'

'Julius, you are so good.'

'Not at all.' He shook his head. 'I'm only doing it for you, Carrie, and as far as I'm concerned, he never deserved you.'

'Well, I'm just glad he has you watching out for him.'

'Enough about your ex, please.' Swiveling about in his chair, he pointed a finger at the blacked-out window behind the desk, and in a loud voice, said, 'Clear.' Immediately, the large window became totally transparent. About a hundred yards distant, a crumbling Buddhist stupa, its dome strung with fluttering prayer flags, occupied the summit of a grassy knoll. It looked out onto a range of snow-capped mountains, which were dominated by a jagged peak.

'Tibet,' Carrie said, the two lines of flags, crossed over the white dome, as a pair of raised eyebrows, reminding her of the way Jake had sometimes looked at her over their breakfast table. Gone.

Misreading her wistful smile as approval, Fatberg trumpeted, 'Ah, for once you are wrong!' He raised a finger. 'It's Nepal.'

'Well, I was close.' Carrie was amused to find him so predictable. 'So, how's the negotiation going with the government there?'

'I've given up on them,' he said, his disappointment written across his face. 'The exchange package deal they were offered on the global outreach program would have dealt with their homeless problem at a stroke.'

'More subs?'

'Of course,' Fatberg nodded, 'ten supersized subs for Kathmandu alone. But perhaps they'll still bite. Their loss if they don't.' He shrugged. 'Elsewhere, however, things are moving fast. Our corporate investors are very pleased with reports from the test subs on the Firebrick site, by our Verity Studios there, and we're just about ready to start rolling out the program across the world.'

'That must make you feel very good.'

'You know what they say,' he sighed, 'every good deed deserves punishment. Frankly, with my track record, that worries me.' He gave a sly smile. 'Carrie, I'm exhausted. I just wish you would join me. There is no one close I can trust and I feel so alone.'

'Julius, I know it sounds petty with all you're doing, but I've been so busy reinstating the apartment, after all the damage. I couldn't have managed without the hazmat team you provided, but still it's been a lot of work.'

'It's finished?'

'Not quite.'

'How long?'

'Soon,' she shrugged. Framed in the 3D box monitor, his pensive face reminded her of a puppy dog, hanging on her every word. 'Another week, I guess,' she said, throwing him a bone.

'And then you'll come out and join me?' he said, insistently. 'Together we can change the world.'

'Julius, I hear you, but I'm only just getting over breaking up with Jake.'

'Wounds heal, and I'm here to make all the hurt go away, you know that Carrie.'

'But where? I'm a homebody, Julius, you must see that. Everyday you're somewhere else. Nepal, Mexico, Ecuador, New Zealand.' She paused. 'And tomorrow?'

'Wherever you want to be, Carrie. It's that simple, just like me.'

She laughed. 'Now that I don't believe.'

'Carrie,' he insisted, 'at heart I'm a simple guy, and with you at my side, to share all I have, I wouldn't want for anything else. Truly.'

Following this exchange, Jake2 concluded that the vehemence of Fatberg's parting remark must have struck a false note with Carrie, who was no fool – unlike his muddle-headed body double at the other end of the triangular configuration of lines, who was conscious again and telegraphing mixed messages he was trying to ignore.

Stepping out of the shower, Jake watched its cubicle recess back into the wall next to the retractable WC and sink, before the sliding panel hid it from sight.

Everything operated just as he had designed. The single bed converted to a surprisingly comfortable chair at the touch of a button. The folding shelving/desk unit offered 22 different configurations. But perhaps best of all was the overhead blacklight projector, which made the walls go away when it turned the cell into a v-center. But no time to play with any of that. The man in the green suit was waiting in the corridor outside, and there was an emergency to deal with.

Unable to contain a sudden uprush of spirits, which was all to do with having recently expressed his iteration and for the first time being free of its nagging shadow, Jake burst into song.

'Happy, happy, to be al-ive-o,
Far better to be stuck in a sub
Than shut-in a lousy apartment
With only your true love for company,
And nowhere particular to go.'

As he ended the call with Carrie, Fatberg reflected that the time had passed when he could unburden himself, as he had hoped to when he first instructed his appointments manager to arrange a session with her.

One thing had led to another, and now it was too late. Just as well, from Carrie's point of view, because had he confessed his secret despite the multifarious binding clauses and penalties specified in their confidentiality agreement, he now belatedly realized, that he couldn't allow her to continue as a therapist – or indeed to continue at all, such was the sad reality of his position as the lifetime CEO and largest shareholder of the biggest corporation in the world. So in that respect at least, he was relieved, not least for having avoided the ensuing unpleasantness he would have had to suffer.

Actually, on reflection, he found he was actually glad, for the amazing thing was that in her he had found the antidote to that old memory which had bugged him for years, because he always forgot about it when in her company. Despite her incredibly irritating habit of objecting to things he said, he found that he positively enjoyed her company. This was perplexing, because the way he saw it people were only there to be used, and any pleasure he got out of them was having them perform as he wanted and receiving their adulation. Of course, there was the fact of her royal bloodline, and the untapped potential of that, which made her even more exclusive than the 1% of the 1% who, in his consideration, were the only people on the planet or off it who counted. But then it occurred to him that here might just be one option, where he could share his secret with her without risk to his – or indeed *her* – security. However, before coming to a decision, obviously first he needed to consult his lawyers.

As he looked out of his window, Fatberg frowned. The NGO intermediary who'd arranged the sale with the head honcho Lama down at the monastery (3021 ft. below), had guaranteed his operations manager that the hilltop site was uninhabited. So how come the crumbling dome of that ruined old building outside was now strung with those dumb little flags, when there had been none on it when he parked the Pizza Hut the night before?

He had only bought the hilltop site for its unobstructed view of K2, a name he rather liked because of the number attached. Presently, he was in negotiations with the Nepalese government to bag the Himalayan mountain, which at 28,248.031496 ft. (a measurement he had confirmed with his state-of–the art altimeter as he flew over it in his Pizza Hut) was the second highest in the world after the mountain with the name he could never remember (its altitude being 29,029.201 ft.). But negotiations to buy both of them had stalled over the compensation demands by the Nepalese Government, which Fatberg considered too steep, despite the prestige and other benefits that ownership would bring him.

In his experience, elected governments were too many-headed to prevail over his singular intent (and great wealth), but he was impatient to conclude the negotiations, which had already dragged on far too long. However, he was confident that the objections to the sale would soon be overcome once their king, who had been deposed in a coup two years before, was back on his throne. It was a development he expected in a matter of days, after the necessary payments to certain parties – army generals and key government ministers to facilitate the change at the top – and their king was once again in residence in his palace.

The way he saw it, the Land ruled the Sea and the Mountains ruled the Land, and so, by owning the highest mountain of all, which he would rename The Fatberg, his supreme position would become abundantly clear to everyone. It was that simple. As in earlier times had been known by pontiffs, caliphs, and other religious leaders, Man was ruled by signs and symbols (now known as brands). In the end these were just trademarks, and therefore property, as long as the copyright of them was protected by a bunch of lawyers. That had been the great discovery made by the corporations in the late twentieth century. And that supreme mountain, which he would make his logos, was the greatest brand of all. Only when it was finally his would he at last be seen for what he really was, without having to endlessly spell it out to all those below, something which he felt went against the grain of his understated personal style.

But what was that annoying hum, outside? Irritated at being brought back down to earth, (even though still at an elevation of 7,082.117 ft. above sea level, that being the altitude he had recorded on his altimeter upon landing the Pizza Hut the night before), Fatberg decided to investigate what was disturbing his peace on his hilltop property.

*

Carrie was in a dilemma about what to do about Jake.

Whatever he was presently going through, he had brought it on himself by a sustained campaign of self-destructive behavior – his repeated violations of Code 307 of the Emergency Regulations being the least of it. But even though she felt betrayed because he had knowingly imperiled her guest status in the city (and therefore their relationship) each time he ventured onto the roof, she still loved him.

But, although he would always have suzerainty over a corner of her heart, she couldn't allow herself to be held hostage a moment longer for a love he had deliberately spurned in his last manic episode and which clearly did not deserve. *Although,* beforehand, he had signed over half of the flat to her – that somehow made it feel worse, because that only proved forethought and that his apparently insane behavior had been a deliberate act. Which, in turn, went to show he'd wanted out of their relationship for months, if not all along, and just couldn't face telling her. His real insanity of course was consciously setting about accruing all those code 307 violations, and getting himself locked up in the subs. How mad was that?

It was obvious she was far better off without him, and that was the hard truth she had to confront in the here-and-now, instead of taking the ostrich option and postponing any decision till when-never. As things had turned out, Jake had been unable to protect her, and it was only through Julius's intervention that she'd survived. And that, as John had always drummed into her, should always be her absolute priority, not just because both her parents and her beloved Grandmama had died so that she might live, but also because she was the last of the Romanov Dynasty, and as such she had a duty to her ancestors to perpetuate her royal bloodline. How when she was younger she had hated him every time he reminded her of all that inheritance shit (as she then had thought of it, while growing up in New Zealand where people rubbed along together and most didn't give a toss for status or position). But now, looking back, she could no longer deny the ring of truth in his forceful words, which she still heard echoing in her head after all these years.

*

This much Jake2 had learned in his limited sojourn in the material world. Those innumerable lines zipping through the air over the city, below where he was on the roof of the Pierspoint building, connected locales, random encounters, affairs, relationships, locales and all manner of events – past, present, and possibly future, though that he had yet to ascertain. Confluences, where lots of lines met, occurred at places of significance: city intersections, subway stations, shopping malls, tall buildings in prominent positions like the Pierspoint, itself a burial site of great importance to the original people, who still haunted that high place, above the great city, and its confluences below where multiple lines met were like watering hoes in the wild, but instead of water, elementals like those he had seen riding the lines supped the energy that gathered there. However, peril lurked in such places, for the nature of the double world was predatory, just as its material counterpart was. He had also discovered that the people of the city had iterations, too, as did their pets.

However, these were less substantive than shadows, and stayed closer. But when asleep and dreaming, their iterations grew more substantial, and sometimes appeared in the streets below, in different states of disapparel, buck naked or in mismatched clothes, confused as to where they were, before just as suddenly disappearing. Back doors, he learned, were everywhere. Mirrors were the easiest to spot. At different times of the day, when the fluxing energies ebbed or surged along the lines, lesser reflective surfaces might become exits and entrances too. Some led nowhere. Others were traps, nasty things lying in wait round blind corners, but some were portals offering glimpses of distant places. People had back doors too, and not just the obvious, also belly button, mouth, nostrils, ear holes, crown of the head, and a point below the point of the big toe of the left foot, worked just as well, though the cranium trapdoor at the back of the skull was harder to prise open.

Of all the people Jake2 tested in the double world, Fatberg's proved the most resistant.

The difficulty he faced was the sheer number of lines passing Fatberg's various backdoors (of which he had no more than any other person) connecting him to people, places, events, and devices. So many indeed radiating Fatberg's backdoors, from the perspective of the double world the lines, a porcupine would have been an apt comparison – only this was one possessed of an infinite number of spines, that extended to the furthest corner of the planet and beyond. Truly, in his physical aspect, the man was a phenomenon. But for Jake2, the biggest puzzle of all was that there didn't seem to be another side to him. Sure he was conniving, duplicitous, and an expert liar – that was evident, in everything he said and did. However, uniquely with Fatberg, what you saw was what you got, and no matter how hard Jake2 had pried, he still hadn't been able to detect so much as a trace of a shadow It lurking in the bristling man.

*

As soon as he stepped down from the Pizza Hut it was obvious to Fatberg that the weird *aumm* sound issued from within the stupa on the summit of the hill. The basso vibration was accompanied by higher frequencies, which set his capped teeth on edge as he walked up the slope towards the whitewashed building, its dome still fluttering with ragged flags, put up without permission, by whoever was making that annoying sound inside.

Perhaps, he speculated, it was a local band, and this was the only place they had to practice their weird *aumm* Nepalese music. Maybe he should pass them onto an A and R producer, on one of his v-record labels? It certainly had something, that deep vibration, impacting his solar plexus, making him feel quite lightheaded as he walked closer. But then, when he was a few feet away from the dark entrance (5 ft., he later estimated) the sound suddenly jumped in volume, and it was like he hit a wall, and he could go no further.

Was it a force-field, he wondered, testing it for breaches with his hands.

Who was responsible? Perhaps it was a secret weapon of the Nepalese Military. If so, he would protest at the highest level to their government. This was his property.

After circling the stupa several times in an anticlockwise direction, and still being kept away by the invisible wall, Fatberg retreated back to his Pizza Hut, to mull the problem over.

Yet he later decided to ignore the stupid stupa, and the dumb Nepalese music, which were only a distraction from his most tricky problem – namely Carrie, and what to do about her ...

*

CHAPTER 2

Batbox conversation on small talk: 02.01. hrs, 9/10/43.

'Hey D'lish, what's new?'

'Not much this end, Grimepappa. Reliving the teens I never had in the latest 90's v-peat, is about it. You?'

'The biggest blockbuster ever! The Great Olympus Games, up on Mount Olympus with the gods.'

'Wow!'

'You have to catch it livestream before it goes to v-ries.'

'Who you playin'?'

'A god.'

'That figures. Who?'

'Prometheuz.'

'Sexy?'

'What do you think? (laughs) He's a god!'

'Handsome?'

'You bet. Total hunk. Superpowers, all

that. You'd love him.'

'Sounds like. When can we meet?'

(laughs) 'He's the youngest god. Real cheeky. Loves his mom but don't get on with his daddy, who's real bad, like you can't imagine. Been great playin' in his skin so far, but won't last I can tell.'

'You reckon?'

'Yea, trouble ahead. Expect, big, black clouds, bubbling up, everywhere, to boil a planet in a hot broth of Flashin' lightnin', crashin' thunder, floods. All that. Yea. My big bad daddy god, beatin' up my sweet mommy god, above those weeping, roiling clouds. Up in Mount Olympus, all my sister gods and brother gods giving me grief, like I'm to blame ...'

Her stiletto heels clicking on the treads of a rolling strip mill designed to replicate the sounds and sensations of movement of any number of environments, Rhea, the Mother of the gods, was very annoyed indeed. The strip mill was, in this case, replicating the flagstones of an echoing passageway leading into a labyrinth of tunnels, cored into a 70,00 foot high non-fungible cliff.

The fact that until recently all the gods in her charge had been unemployed actors subsisting on BRED was neither here nor there. Until you stepped off set (passed through that that minor delirium no one ever admitted to), while in character they were gods and should act accordingly, and not go off-script, as one of them just had. Livestream verities were as real as you made them, and belief was the most important constituent in passing on that special shared 'reality' to the audience, who after all became participants in real-time, or whenever they replayed the verity.

She was angry because the actor playing her young son Prometheuz had refused to go against the will of Zeus, the father of the gods. Even as a child, Zeus was a monster, when but a little boy he killed both of his parents, the last of the Titans, so ending their reign in heaven. Then, becoming a father, he devoured the first eight of their children soon as they were born, standing, grinning at her, smacking his ruddy lips behind his bloodied beard, after snacking on their tender flesh like they were suckling piglets, belching and spitting out their chewed bones (which ever after circled Heaven, far out beyond the orbit of Saturn, later known as the Cuiper Belt of asteroids and occasionally raining down judgement on unsuspecting mortals). That was before she made the tunnel labyrinth, where she hid when giving birth. The birth chamber itself was located in his one blind spot, directly below his throne on the lofty summit of Mount Olympus, from where he surveyed the whole of creation.

At a relatively safe distance from Zeus's terrible rages, but conveniently placed in Rhea's view, lay the nursery planet where infant immortals were confined until of an age to fend for themselves in Olympus. There, sibling rivalry was fierce. Being the youngest god by several millennia, Prometheuz, although no longer an infant, had the planet all to himself. As such, none of his older sisters or brothers were around to warn him not to breathe life into the manikins he had shaped from clay-dough in the play pit which, in a far distant future, would be known as Africa. The new creatures were fast breeders, and before long they were spreading across the small world, trailing destruction behind them.

When Zeus heard what Prometheuz had done, he was furious. Breath was life, and by bestowing his on these creatures he had given them consciousness, which up till then had been an attribute of the gods alone.

But Prometheuz, who was the most stubborn of Zeus's children, then enraged his father still further, by pleading to be allowed to give his new playmates fire because it was cold down in the nursery, and the little humans, as he called the creatures he had created, did not have the means to heat themselves.

Zeus had heard enough. Summoning all the gods to his great hall, he then issued one of his famous edicts.

'Fire,' he thundered, 'is the sole property of the gods, for it is one of the four sacred elements from which everything is composed. The knowledge of how to make it must remain ours and ours alone, till the end of eternity. For should these vermin which Prometheuz has willfully created, or any other mortal creature, ever learn the secrets of making the sacred element, then at some time distant in the future Olympus itself might be overthrown.'

He paused, noticing that pillars of the hall had started shaking, threatening to bring the vast roof crashing down on the bowed heads of the assembled gods. Moderating his tone slightly, he continued, 'This I have seen in the tapestry of the heavens, which as every god knows contains all possible pasts and futures, in the weft and woof of the omnipresent-verse.'

But that was precisely the outcome Rhea most fervently desired. And so, when her youngest son, Prometheuz, upon whom her hopes of liberation from the rule of her despotic husband now depended, refused her secret command to steal fire from the sacred flame which perpetually flickered in the hearth of Zeus's Great Hall, she didn't know what to do. The prospect of submitting to her husband's will forever and ever, which meant being regularly raped in their marital bed, or elsewhere for that matter, then bearing an endless succession of children who only grew up to despise her, was one she could not countenance.

And besides, unless Prometheuz did as he was told, there would be no story, no blockbuster verity telling of the twilight of the gods, followed by the rise and fall and rise again of humanity. It was the building of civilizations from Gilgamesh, Nineveh, Babylon, and ziggurats of Mesopotamia, when Sargon ruled the Middle East, the Pyramids in Egypt, the ancient Greeks, the empire of Alexander the Great, Carthage and the Punic wars, with the Roman empire, the Tang dynasty in China, the corresponding civilizations in the Americas, the European renaissance, the Industrial Revolution, before the modern age, and rise of the American Empire, and the great digital age that elevated the super-rich to titan status, at last bringing the epic up-to-date, when one Titannaire would consume all the others and the great cosmic cycle could begin again. Without it, all the actors, herself included, would all too soon be again subsisting on BRED, a prospect she could not abide.

Whereas, for Prometheuz, who, if he agrees, in the next episode will be sentenced by his father to be chained to a rock on Mount Caucusus on planet Earth, where he played as a child. There he would have his liver eaten by an eagle by day, only for it to regrow overnight and endure the same, in the following X number of episodes of the livestream verity. It was a prospect he could not, *would not*, agree to, as he had made abundantly clear to his divine mother.

The new inductee was perfect for the part, the producer and the team all agreed, but only after they got the message without being told – that no more delay will be tolerated…

So it was decided, on a whim and nod at the very top, descending through the vital but nevertheless non-specific order descending the 10 C-title ranks of corporate structure, from the Chief executive officer, to the Chief of Information Officer, then via the Board, to Chief of Staff, the Vice Chairman, Director, Associate Director, Vice Presidents, and down through the 20 subdivisions of Middle Management.

It was passed on, in shrugs and winks, sometimes with words appended to flesh out body language, till it was finally received and understood well enough, though not without a few grumbles from the bottom feeders behind the scenes. But no matter. Despite the new player's obvious total lack of experience, and grumbles aside, the production team were all compliant and got on with preparations for the next episode without protest. For every link in that corporate command chain knew that to do otherwise would have damaged their career prospects across an integrated network of companies, most being prime movers in their respective fields of commerce and industry – whether in construction, housing, property management, insurance, finance and debt recovery, autonomous delivery and transport, satellite launchers, virtual travel, news and entertainment (which of course came under the new heading of V-media), citizen security, remote policing, homeless welfare, and enforcing the provision of the new universal mental health legislation. Such was the connectivity of the giant corporation across the piste, as the saying went in the shut-in world.

*

Jake frowned. As far as he remembered, the schemata of the subs, which he'd worked on for all those months, only had 12 levels, yet the illuminated panel above the shiny steel doors had just signaled 13, indicating that the rapid transit elevator was still descending.

'Not much further now,' George George said, perhaps sensing Jake's confusion.

'How deep does this go?' Jake said, as the elevator slowed and 23 glowed on the screen.

'All the way!' George George said, with a shudder. 'Believe me, you don't want to know. The lower levels,' he added, pointing a finger down at the floor, 'have been reserved for our more hopeless cases.

Fortunately,' he smiled lopsidedly, 'presently, we don't have too many of those, but that will change.'

'I see,' Jake said, becoming more confused as the doors opened onto a vast space.

Dim illumination was provided by emergency lighting panels spaced at hundred or so yard intervals along the intensely black walls. The dim light from below reflected off the undersides of a multitude of shiny rails, which with his architectural knowledge Jake instantly recognized as the latest in malev lighting tracks, which were suspended from a network of gantries high above. The floor below was scattered with equipment, the purpose of most of which he could only guess at. Some four hundred yards distant, as far as he could judge, halfway between the two walls to the side, a raised circular area occupying the center of the space suggested a stage, on which were free-standing L-shapes, curves, and half-circles, that appeared to be constructed with the same light-absorbing material as the walls were.

'Fabulous, isn't it!' George George said into the vastness, which seemed to swallow his voice, like ink spilled on blotting paper, with no reverb whatsoever from the distant walls.

'But what is it?' Jake said, peering into the darkness, which seemed to stretch infinitely ahead.

'What you are looking at, Mr Cousins,' George George beamed, lopsidedly, 'is only the biggest, the best, the most costly and futuristic verity studio in the whole world.'

'But why so large?'

'Aha!' George George raised a long finger, knobbly and bent, 'Very good question, Mr Cousins. That's so it can accommodate a cast of thousands.'

'How is that legal,' Jake interjected, 'when for the past three years under the emergency regulations meetings of more than two people have been forbidden?'

'There are always exemptions, Mr Cousins,' George George assured him, blandly.

'Such as?' Jake insisted.

'Well, the subs, as you call them,' George George said, seemingly surprised by the question.

'That's only because they provide emergency housing,' Jake snapped. 'But this...' He gestured at the surroundings. 'This is to do with the entertainment industry. There's no exemption for that, surely.'

'Aha,' George George wagged that finger, 'but the regulations only extend sixty feet below ground, or three floors, whichever is greater. As the esteemed designer of the, ah, subs, I had assumed you would be aware of that.'

'But what about the dangers of the dust, for instance those manic attacks people can have after inhaling it.' Jake, who up to then had been a sceptic about the potential side-effects, was suddenly wondering if inhaling the toxic dust during his one or other of his excursions on the roof of the Pierspoint, had brought on his recent episode (forgetting of course, he'd only been an onlooker, as his iteration smashed every device in apartment).

'Be reassured, Mr Cousins, at this depth below ground, and breathing charcoal-filtered air as we are, there is, ah, no particulate risk whatsoever posed by the deadly Siberian dust. We are entirely safe here, I promise, which would not be the case obviously if, ha hah, the studio were, um, above ground.'

'I have understood that,' Jake said, becoming impatient with George George's long winded explanations. 'Please, could you expand about this cast of thousands.'

'Ah yes, the cast. Well, ah, first there is the actual cast, the ah, real-live actors, so to speak, and then there is the, um crowd of, um, avatars, I believe that is the correct name?'

'The perps,' Jake said, more to himself.

'The what?' George George peered intently at Jake.

'Sorry, of course I mean the avatars.'

'Indeed,' George George nodded gravely.

'Where do they go?' Jake insisted.

'Is it not obvious?' George George expostulated, 'in the stands, of course.'

'What stands? I don't see any,' Jake said, making a show of peering around.

'Oh they are projected.' George George waved a hand, airily. 'Nothing to write home about. Like any amphitheater, but on a scale to accommodate billions only the ascending tiers are each divided into enclosures, which are opened at the end of the show. The stage is in the middle, over there.' He pointed. 'But there is no proper set, as you might expect in a play or a movie, just crosses and grids marked on the floor, and the ah higgledy piggledy structures that the technicians tell me will be granite furniture, temple walls, and altars, and so forth.' He paused, and turned towards Jake. 'Am I going on too long?' He swept back a lank lock of hair that had fallen over his eyes. 'It's a bad habit of mine, I'm told.' He looked down.

'I guess V-tech production is *confusing,'* Jake said, glad he had stopped himself before saying 'alarming', and suppressing a desire to laugh.

George George sighed. 'Things were much more straightforward in my time, and of course done very differently. However I do understand that these days the participating avatars prime the pump, so to speak, and are considered essential to the financing of big production serials.' He raised a finger. 'But that is when the, ah, subs, enter the picture.'

'I was wondering when you'd get round to that.' Jake smiled.

'Yes, we provide real-life extras, when needs be,' George George said, with evident pride. 'Also, when needed, a back-up crew, as it were, who assist all the support staff that livestream big budget verities require nowadays.'

'But there's no one here,' Jake said, looking around to make a point.

'That's because they are, ah, preparing for the next episode, Mr Cousins.'

'So where is this emergency you need my help with?' Jake said, with the odd thought that the studio was the same number of floors below ground as the roof of the Pierspoint was above it.

'That, I have to admit, Mr Cousins,' George George said, squinting down his nose sheepishly at him, 'was just a ploy to get you down here.' He smiled lopsidedly. 'So what do you think?'

'Great.' Jake shrugged, realizing that he was only 23 floors underground because of all his code 307 violations up on the roof, where he'd inhaled the toxic dust, in another life which was now fading like a dream. 'Very impressive, yea. But I don't know what it has to do with me.'

'Ah ha.' George George raised a finger. 'But that's where you are wrong,' he said, emphatically. 'This has *everything* to do with you.' He shook his head, sadly. 'If only I was younger, I might have had stood an outside chance.' He sighed, deeply. 'But instead, they have chosen you.' He extended a hand. 'Truly, it is, ah, the greatest honor of my life to be the first to congratulate you on your, ah, marvelous good fortune.' Overdoing the dramatics, George George placed his other hand over his heart. 'Believe me when I say that I shall always remember this moment.'

Observing the exchange from a distant location, Jake2 smiled darkly to himself, knowing full well what came next for his unfortunate body double.

*

CHAPTER 3

Conversation on the FauxReel Culture Vultures Channel: 15:hrs. 11/10/43.

'Elliot, is that really you under that basket of writhing snakes?'

'Yes Petronella, it truly is. I have finally changed my allegiances from avian to monster. This is my new avatar. Humungous doesn't begin to address the new Me, don't you think?'

'Ghastly! I hardly dare look.'

'Afraid of being turned to stone?'

'Hardly! That would make me a Roc.'

'Very funny. I'm in character, for the next episode. Two hours to go. I can't wait.'

'Me too, though I can't see what connection Medusa of the Perseus legend has with Prometheuz.'

'Oh come on, the Ancient Greeks were always mixing their myths. You know that.'

'That's like conflating Adam and Eve

with Samson and Delilah, which I think you'll find I am correct in saying comes three hundred and twenty-two chapters on in the Bible.'

'You always were so picky, Petronella.'

'Just making a point, Elliot. Prometheuz and his conflict with his almighty father, Zeus, was the Ancient Greeks' creation myth, just as for us the legend of the Fall is, in the Old Testament.'

'Testament, now that's an interesting word, don't you think?'

'So like you to try changing the subject when you know I'm right, Elliot.'

'Not at all, Petronella. Testament is derived from testicle, because no one believed those Biblical Patriarchs unless they cupped theirs when swearing oaths. The word's absolutely fundamental to Western Civilization.'

'Maybe for you, Elliot, but certainly not for me!

'You are so right, Petronella. Vultures like you don't have 'em!'

*

Concealed by thick smog, the Pizza Hut's containment field's stabilizers, embedded in its seven sides, ensured the craft remained more or less stationary at 15.3 feet above the building, with a deviation either side of just 0.012 inches, as measured by the on-board optical instrumentation as it hovered over the roof of the Pierspoint.

However, unusually, Fatberg wasn't thinking of any of that, nor did he pause to consider as he descended the steps – or even to count them as otherwise habitually he would have done – that in a FauxReel studio, 23 levels under the Firebrick site, the much-heralded livestream episode, coincidentally also numbered 23, of the biggest blockbuster was about to begin. Instead, he was anxiously wondering what sort of reception awaited him in the apartment directly below.

When Carrie heard the ceiling hatch in the hall outside her workroom sliding back, then saw the roof ladder extending towards the floor, she thought she was dreaming. Jake was locked away in the subs, so how come he was clambering down the ladder, into the apartment? But then, with a flash of anger, she recognized who it was.

'Julius, how the hell …?' 'Please.' He held up his hands. 'I only had one chance to come here without being observed and that is today, when everyone's attention is elsewhere.'

'And what's so special about today?' she demanded, hands on hips, glowering.

'Only the biggest grossing verity of all time.' He glanced at his watch, paused, then looked up. 'In precisely nine minutes and twenty seconds, the two singing comperes will start the countdown to episode twenty-three of the Great Olympus Games show, or the GO Games as it has become known.'

'Oh that.' Carrie shrugged. 'I never participate.'

'Billion already are, just everyone in the city will be streaming – apart from you.' He laughed, covering up his nervousness, before adding, in a pleading tone, 'And me.'

'Hmm.' Carrie, who was not long out of the shower and still in her dressing gown, uncrossed her arms and relaxed her stance. 'Well, it's good to have you here at last, Julius.' She half smiled. 'But I still don't understand why you couldn't give me some warning.'

'It was a last minute snap decision I could only make when I could be sure that the smog had thickened enough to conceal the hut from being seen from below.'

'Ok, I finally understand.' Smiling, she spread her arms and motioned with her hands. 'Come on, give me a hug. I think I need it as much as you do, Julius.'

*

'Please try not to move, you need to let these gorgeous rectus abdominis muscles settle-in or they won't bond properly, Prometheuz, sir.'

'How many times do I have to tell you, my name is Cousins, not Prometheuz,' Jake protested, weakly.

'Of course, Mr, ah, Cousins,' the body therapist hastily corrected herself, as she leaned over him. 'It's just with these muscles, I can't help thinking of you as Prometheuz, who I have followed from the beginning. I admit I was totally devastated when I heard the last actor had walked out on the set. But quite honestly I find you so much more impressive, and I know that you'll soon win the audience over.' She sighed happily as she applied creams to his tender new flesh, of what he had previously thought of as his abs, as he lay, a mask on his face, under the bright lights of the make-up suite, into which he had been wheeled, strapped to the cantilevered bed, some minutes before.

'May I say they've done a tremendous job in the Lab. This maximus glutinous is absolutely outstanding,' she went on, carefully avoiding the prominent bump of his gauze-wrapped genitals, which were particularly tender, moving her hands down to his thighs. 'Since I began here, Mr Prom –sorry, Mr Cousins – seven months ago, though it seems an age, just before the first sensational episode of The First Family when Zeus ate the triplet godlings his poor wife had just given birth to and the whole world got hooked, I've made-up all the Olympians, who all went through the same procedure, and let me tell you, none of them looked half so god-like after their ordeal ...'

As she chattered on, this time about the distortion lenses they projected on the set, Jake was desperately trying to recall one of the bedtime stories his grandfather had read to him from the Book of Greek Legends when he was a small child. But it was no use. Despite his best efforts, the details of what happened to the hero escaped him. He needed to remember in order to work out what came next. But his lines the silly voice coach (who confusingly kept calling him Prometheuz) had recited to him earlier, all the time looping round the wheelchair in her rollerblades while an orderly, who he never saw pushed him up the ramp, told him very little. Besides, the words she had made him endlessly repeat were all jumbled up in his head by the time they reached the top, where a lizard lawyer in a sharp suit, with creases that could have cut paper, stood waiting before rubber double doors under a sign that said 'GENOPLAST' in ominous black letters.

From the moment the lawyer took over from the voice coach, who skated away back down the spiral ramp way to the Induction Suite from whence they had just come, lizard legalese never stopped coming out of the near side of the lawyer's motor mouth. He went on about minutiae of a contract which Jake was now required to understand, though he only made out about one word in three, and understood even less, they came so fast. Without a let-up of the monologue, the lawyer wheeled Jake through the door and into a blue-lit room, where he was told to strip off by a white-coated technician and made to stand against a wall marked with a grid, while different-coloured lights from a hidden source in the ceiling played over his naked body, as another technician traced dotted lines projected onto his skin, outlining different areas of his anatomy, back and front, which most worryingly included his groin, with a big felt-tipped pen.

The only details of the contract that he could now remember, after the 7-hour procedure he had just undergone, were the seven zeros of the 9-figure number, which had made him quite dizzy, when he'd read them. The money to be transferred into an off-shore bank account which had already been opened in his name immediately upon his completing his part in the last episode of the First Family series.

But then, after he signed on the 40th page of the densely worded contract and it had been witnessed by one of the technicians, the lawyer's tone had changed from silk to sandpaper, as he spoke of the dire consequences of being found to be intoxicated while on the set, or, worst of all, if he walked out on and broke his contract, as his predecessor in the role had. In that case, the most egregious penalties of the 192 sanctions as set out in the many sub-clauses of the contract would be applied with the utmost rigor, by the battery of L.A. lawyers which FauxReel kept on hand for just such an eventuality.

With the lawyer's final warning ringing in his ears, and escorted by a honor guard of white-coated technicians, he was propelled upon a trolley through the next set of double doors under a sign that said 'THEATRE' in bold black letters, and into a vast white space which was ablaze with lights, where the purpose of all those mysterious red-dotted lines marked on his anatomy finally became clear.

*

Standing with her back to him, Carrie studied his reflection in the kitchen mirror. Sitting with his hands clenched on the tabletop before him, he was pretending to look around the room, while covertly casting her side glances.

'Black or white?' she cast back over her shoulder.

'Black, please,' he said, their eyes meeting in the mirror, 'I never take it any other way.'

'Sugar?' she asked, smiling.

'No, never.' He laughed nervously. 'Too many calories. I stopped taking it twenty-three months and …'

Leaning around him, she laid a coaster on the table before him and placed the steaming mug of coffee on top. Standing behind him, her dressing gown brushing his back as she kneaded his shoulders, she said, 'Julius, you're *so* tense.'

'It's been a hard week,' he sighed. 'I've left the team to carry on the negotiation in that dumb cat capital. Sorry, I forget its name. The whole time that spooky monk aumm music playing somewhere. Take it from me, all Neps are nuts. You cannot imagine how stupid ...'

'Julius, forget all that,' she said, settling in her chair. 'You're here.' Reaching over the table and grasping his hands, she unclenched his fingers. 'Safe. With me.'

She settled back in her chair, and regarded him coolly. 'Julius,' she continued, 'you never do anything without a reason, I know, so please tell me what's on your mind.' She arched an elegant eyebrow. 'Unless of course you've lost it, and you really did come all this way for my coffee? I know it's good but not that good, surely.'

'Carrie, I ...' Caught in the spell of her glittering peacock blue eyes, he was unable to look away.

'Go on,' she urged.

'I've been so lonely I ...' His downcast eyes welled, self-piteously.

'Listen, Julius, I won't be able to respect you as a man if you can't tell me. You need to know that. I'm just that sort of woman.'

'Carrie I …' Suddenly, Fatberg knelt before her. 'Carrie, please, will you consent to be my wife. I promise …' He gulped, perspiration peppering his forehead. 'I swear, I will always care for you.'

Intent, she studied his upturned face, secretly glad that at least he hadn't mentioned love because, as she had lately learned, that only got in the way of survival in a cruel world. Knowing she was losing Jake in that moment, she took a deep breath, and smiled.

'Yes.' She clasped the hand which Julius extended. 'But on one condition.'

'Condition?' – *was that a petulant frown, Jake2, who was remote viewing the scene, wondered.*

'Our marriage must be kept secret.'

'But I imagined …'

'No, Julius, the ceremony has to be totally private. There must be no press intrusion whatsoever or you can forget it.'

'I agree! Yes, totally, absolutely!' he exclaimed, jumping to his feet.

'In that case, Julius, you may now kiss me.'

Watching from afar and near, Jake2 was pleased.

Now that their lifelines, on which he had been focused, were twined and soon to be knotted, at last he could advance his plans in other directions. Since he had come into actualized existence he had learned that any form of stasis, such as he had just endured to bring together the two people in the apartment below where he was bi-located, sitting cross-legged on the old rooftop watertank, posed innumerable risks for him, just as they would any of the other elementals who flitted between the double world and its earthly counterpart. They were half-life beings, which like him were composed of more energy than substance and were never one thing nor another, but so much more free than the shut-in denizens of either world.

CHAPTER 4

The PERP-VOX PEEP Show-*Scoops all the poop between the scenes.*

'Oh there you are, Petronella, dearest. With so many of your kind here today, it was hard to make you out in that flock.'

'I would have spotted you anywhere in that ghastly hissing headdress. And anyway, Elliot, or should I say, *my dear* Medusa, the correct term for a gathering of more than three vultures is "kettle".'

'I never knew that, would you credit it?'

'Yes, I would. Before you turned feather, you were always a most laggardly raptor.'

'Really?'

'Yes, and besides, I was in a minority of one over there.'

'So my new snake eyes were deceiving me, were they?'

'Aside from the fact I was chatting to one of the three bald eagles in the carrion stand, I believe I am correct in saying I am the only representative of my ancient genus of vulture here today.'

'And what is that, pray?'

'The nephhron percnioptrous genus, more commonly known as the Egyptian Vulture.'

'Thank you for enlightening me at last, dearest.'

'These days, we are quite rare, you know.'

'Yes, I can see that.'

'We were worshipped as divine in Ancient Egypt.'

'I am sure you were, Petronella. And got to eat pharaohs' entrails too, I imagine.'

'Only after their other body parts had been properly mummified.'

'Of course. And today?'

'We live in hope, my dear Medusa, but with so many pay-2-perp avatars present, I am afraid I don't rate my chances highly, if at all.'

'Tsk, tsk, Petronella. Such gloom is not at all like you. I am sure the other vultures will save you a juicy morsel or two.'

'I wouldn't for them, so why should they?'

'Not even for a divine nephhron percnioptrous?'

'Absolutely not. That would be to forego half the pleasure.'

'More than the ravening and tearing?' *(sighs)* 'I used to love that.'

'Perhaps not, but even so, flying away with the last gibbet in one's beak is always particularly satisfying.'

'Quite so.' *(looks up)* 'Ah, but do I detect the lights are finally dimming?'

'I do believe you are correct, yes. And look at those screens. No, not over there, Elliot, that direction.' *(points a wingtip)* 'At last the colonnades of Olympus are pixelating into view. About time. And the stars of Heaven twinkling beyond. Do you see, on the screens there?'

'Ah, so they are. Marvellous. As always, dearest, your eyesight is spot on.'

'None better. Certainly I wouldn't trust any of yours.' *(laughs)*

'But only my looks can turn to stone, dearest.'

'Not my prey, please, dear Medusa.'

'I wouldn't dare.' *(laughs)* 'Well, to our separate places then, Petronella dearest.'

'Please give my regards to your new kin in the monster stand.'

'Will do, oh divine one, and most assuredly my fellow gorgons will be delighted to receive them. See you after the show, offal permitting.' *(laughs, walks away)*

*

In the Observation Deck, leaning on the rail, Carrie peered down at the roof of the Pierspoint, as it was swallowed by smog.

Would she ever see Jake again, she wondered? Given recent events, she doubted it. Fate, in her experience, was cruel far more often than it was kind. The great wheel of fortune she remembered so vividly from her Granmama's worn deck of cards had turned, and what they'd had would never return – not in this life, anyway, she reflected, not now she was on her way to her secret wedding in Kathmandu.

The past three years with Jake had been the most stable period in her whole life, and the apartment the first real home she'd ever known. Amazingly, despite the long shut-in and her terror whenever the building swayed in the wind, and the fear that never left her because of the height of the tower block, she'd actually been happy most of the time, even though Jake was the most annoying person she'd ever known. But of all his behaviours his foolish arrogance in believing that he could forever get away with flouting the emergency regulations had finally brought disaster down on both of them, and now he was suffering the consequences for his escapes onto the roof.

In a way she blamed herself for not coming down harder on him when she first discovered what he was up to and nipping his behaviors in the bud. But then, reconsidering, she realized he had been hell-bent all along and she could have done nothing to stop him. Poor Jake, how he hated to be confined.

Sobbing silently, she tried to conjure his face out of the fog, knowing then that, despite her anger, she still loved him. What was he thinking of, locked in his cell at that moment? Was he regretting what he had done? Or was he relieved to be free of her nagging, which he was always complaining of, and glad to be finally shot of her? Wiping away the great fat tear that suddenly coursed down her cheek, she wondered if she would ever know happiness again.

Don't look back, never look back, she told herself, steeling herself against the almost overwhelming compulsion to break down and sob her eyes out lest Julius, up in the cockpit, overhear her. She stared into the smog which had swallowed up her past with Jake so completely. Don't look back, never look back. Yea, John's mantra during her childhood years, when to keep ahead of the bad guys they had to move every couple of months, and move countries every two or three years, till they reached New Zealand, after which there was nowhere else to go.

But despite all his care and the precautions he took, they still got him in the end. Then, twelve years later, when she thought they had lost the trail, and she was safe at last, they would have killed her too if Julius hadn't been watching over her. If only he could have warned her about the danger earlier – but even so, he deserved her loyalty, for without his presence of mind at the time and placing those two guard bots in the corridor outside the apartment, she'd be well dead by now. Jake too, since he was standing before her and would have opened the door to the assassin. Too bad he went mad after and wrecked the apartment. But at least by so doing, he decisively ended their relationship, leaving her no other alternative than to go forwards without him.

Though Julius was a cold fish, he clearly cared. But even more importantly considering her perilous present situation, he was rich and powerful enough to protect her from the malevolent force that had been behind the murder of three generations of her family, which she had no doubt still had her in its sights. That the assassins were only instruments of a dark design had long been obvious to her, but now she wasn't even convinced there was a human face in the center of its web, which she sensed was alien in what she could only think of as its essential *wrongness*. Not just her entire family had been wiped out to advance its plans of world domination and total subjection of the planet's entire population. In its name (if indeed it had a name), empires had been toppled, terrible wars had been waged on land and sea and in every corner of the world (and soon above it, if the stand-off in space between the great powers broke down, as looked increasingly likely, and the recent militarization of the lunar surface was anything to go by), while in Russia tens of millions had been murdered, whether by starvation, in forced marches, frozen in Siberian gulags, injected by doctors with weird serums, in medical experiments, or tortured to death by brutal militia, state thugs or soft-spoken KGB killers.

In China too, the story had been much the same under Mao's reforming zeal, except there, if anything, the death toll had been even greater, during the 'great leap forwards' of the 1970's. It was a game, Granmama had explained, which was played by both ends against the middle, where the people always lost no matter which side won. Just as in World War II, at the conclusion of which allegiances and the uniforms changed but the rules stayed the same, and the principal victors remained hidden behind the scenes. Blood-sucking Capitalism and Communism, she said, were bedfellows as hard to tell apart as any two fleas under a blanket.

Considering any of the previous, self-pity wasn't even an option. She was who she was, and if she wanted to retain any self-respect, ultimately she had no choice but to accept the role that history had placed on her shoulders. Like it or not she was the Tsarina, and now that, by proposing, Julius had pledged his implicit support in her cause, who was she to argue against him or indeed the prayers of her long-suffering subjects, whom Granmama had often spoke of. Ever since she remembered, their wrinkled faces had intruded in her dreams, the mad mystics with burning eyes and great flowing white beards, always with crosses on the long black robes they wore over hair shirts, and their mortified flesh they regularly scourged with flails – if Granmama was to be believed. The ragged bent old women in headscarves, shawls slung across bony shoulders, down on their knees on slabs of cold stone, bowing before icons of saints, and heretics in the dimness of onion-domed churches in old Mother Russia, where she had never been, but which was always at the back of her mind. Yea, all those poor oppressed people she had too long turned her back on, their pleading voices following her down the years as, seeking anonymity, she hid, tried to blend into the background wherever she was.

But now, with the clarion call of destiny resounding more urgently than ever in the depths of her being, perhaps she should actually be grateful to Jake for pushing her towards it. Instead of nursing resentments, she should let him go. People weren't possessions, and love that didn't turn into contentment never lasted, always turned to poison. Didn't Granmama tell her that? Or maybe it was something she read somewhere. Whatever, the words rang true. She needed to release the caged bird of their love tangled in her heart-strings and set Jake free, for if she did not the black seeds already lodged there would bear bitter fruit in the years to come. Besides, though not in name, she was the Tsarina in her mind already, if she was honest with herself, so what choice did she have?

Ping went the heart-string, as her connection with Jake finally snapped. She never saw that, but her iteration – the yet-to-be Tsarina of her secret dreams – did.

Jake2, who had dropped in on Carrie and her secret self from where he was bi-located in the Great Hall of Zeus, watched the poor heartstring's fraying end whiplashing away as it spiraled into the infinite depths of a shimmering vortex and vanished into null-time. He would have liked to have shared how it looked from his perspective, but there was no point, neither Carrie nor her iteration would have registered anything, trapped as they were in the world of blinding reflections where, no matter where you are, nothing is as it seems except, sometimes, what is glimpsed in fleeting impressions, or gleaned in dreams.

*

THE GREAT OLYMPUS GAMES –
SCENE # 2 EPISODE 23

Waiting at the foot of the stairs, listening to the yells and catcalls of the restive crowd above, muscle-weary after his genoplast transformation from man into god, Prometheuz, as Jake was now starting to think of himself, had an attack of the shakes. Despite the repeated assurances from his body therapist, and his rollerblading voice coach, he doubted he would ever get used to the added mass of his sore new muscles. Even the short walk from the cosmetic suite to below the stage had exhausted him.

'Fuck this shit,' he cursed as the insistent clamor climaxed in a rabid roar followed by tidal waves of chanting, peaking, crashing from all sides, on the stage of fake dreams.

'PROM! PROM! PROM! PROM! PROM! PROM! PROM!'

The raucous chanting climaxed in a colossal wall of sound. His head bowed, Prometheuz stepped up onto the stage. Then, registering that the new chants of "GO-PROM GO! GO-PROM-GO! GO-PROM-GO" were directed at him, he flung up his hands, receiving the adulation of the pay-2-perps he could just make out beyond the great pillars of Zeus's great hall, which marked the division of light into darkness. Four times he wheeled about, muscles rippling; the roars only got louder, and as he moved his head to face in a new direction, the non-fungible pillars in his line of sight flickered.

He also registered the same effect in his peripheral vision, where the flicker revealed the giant furniture to be non-fungibles positioned on props.

Not so the pay-2-perp avatars packed into the steep stands, none of whom noticed a single flicker in the beamed blacklight-distorting fields, in between the pillars, which were distorting lenses, basically, which in deft perspective shifts ensured no pillar was ever in the way. The zoom function of the distortion field brought the action closer to the perps live-streaming in their v-consoles who were afforded a 360-view of any god or thing anywhere on the vast stage brought right up to their eyes, simply by willing the command to a sender in their headsets, a trick which was soon acquired after a few ejaculations, when masturbating during gory scenes.

Within the ring of towering pillars, the benches of the defense and prosecution were arranged in a half-circle facing the dock isolated in the middle, in turn dwarfed by the high chair of the judge, the fleece of a golden ram, draped over the back. There was a granite gravel resting on the broad right arm of the empty high chair, which, like the rest of the monumental furniture, was cut from massive blocks of polished stone of an inky blackness that seemed to possess infinite depths. The only exceptions to this stone rule: a great bronze sword and a pair of golden shackles attached to the chunky links of a coil of a solid gold chain on the table next to a massive mace, which was big as a plank, only it was round and had a great crystal boss at one end, of a green that seemed supernatural, its glittering depths drew the eye so.

'Great great entrance, Bro,' someone said, from behind. Turning his head in the direction, Prometheuz spotted a big satyr, who seemed familiar somehow and was stuffed into a lurid green body suit two sizes too small for his gangly frame, striding up to him, wearing the red cloak of a public defender slung over his cuirass and armored shoulder.

Most of the gods Prometheuz had seen so far, wore togas, and none exposed hairy knees and gold hooves. From what he knew of the script he guessed this was supposed to be his older brother in Olympus, and the god of inebriation, fertility, and secret pleasures.

'Bro, I'm   DPD that's Dionysus P Dionysus, your ah court appointed defence attorney. Never mind the P.' Dionysus shrugged, 'our mother and her fancies,' he grinned lopsidedly.

'It would help if I knew what I'm charged with,' Prometheuz, managed, helpless with the god's spade hand gripping his bicep, as he was propelled down an aisle between the rows of benches.

'Oh, Zeus's usual trumped-up nonsense,' Dionysus said with difficulty, stooping slightly as he reached two grimy fingernails into his mouth, and pried out a quid of black shag of which he had a regular supply from a dwarf. 'Believe me Bro,' hc said, 'there's no fucking case to answer.' Still firmly gripping Prometheuz by the arm, he palmed the gunk into his other hand and slapped it to the back of a bench, as they passed. Straightening up with a wince, he turned his head, and grinned at a statuesque God standing with a trident among a group of demi-gods, settling in further along the bench.

The giant with the trident had little wriggling electric fish tangled in his flowing purple hair, which might have been seaweed, Jake thought, but at that distance it was hard to tell. He had a great beard, with green streaks, down to his knees, boots so deep they could have been pacific lagoons, tropical fish about his knees, as Jake would have expected, since this was obviously the god Poseidon before him, with a seaweed cape slung stylishly across a great shoulder. He was giving Jake the once over.

The eyes of a god can shoot daggers.

'The charge is totally trumped up, and beyond ridiculous!' Dionysus said, his back armored against just such a look, steering Prometheuz in a new course towards the dock directly under Zeus's high chair.

'But what am I charged with?'

Ignoring the question, Dionysus went on, 'And now, with that great entrance, and winning over the crowd which is always half of the battle, Bro, it's positively guaranteed I'll get you off. I fucking swear, believe me, no matter what that stone-eyed fucker up there has planned for you.' Shielding the gesture with his body, Dionysus thumbed towards the high chair, which Prometheuz noticed was now occupied by the massive bulk of a shadowy robed figure with a great head of curly hair, a long beard, and penetrating gleaming eyes that projected ruby-red rays, which he felt as burning heat on his chest as the Father of the Gods glowered down at him.

*

'Change of plan,' Fatberg announced, looking round as Carrie stepped up into the cabin from her suite of rooms on the second deck. 'You'll never guess where now,' he said, with a sly grin, dismissing his scaled-down Appointments Manager with a flick of his fingers.

'I thought you had arranged everything in Kathmandu,' she said, her eyes drawn to the penitent pinstriped avatar, on his little pedestal, which was a cheap non-fungible of St. Theodore's Column outside St. Mark's in Venice, shrinking to nothingness along with his pedestal in a disappearing cone of blacklight, which blipped off in a dot, making her blink. 'I've always wanted to see the Himalayas,' she said, closing her eyes, still seeing the after-image of the dot burning a hole in her retinas.

'We can go there after.' He patted the one other seat next to his in the timber-lined cabin, which was surprisingly small, given the generous space elsewhere in the craft. 'You'd best strap in,' he said, leaning over the lighted instrument panel, 'the forecast is thick smog below, with atmospheric pressure dropping to 12 millibars, and visibility at ground level between 3.5 and 4.2 feet, so we may hit turbulence as we descend.'

Irritated by the sudden change of direction, and still more by his habit of slipping numbers into the conversation that meant nothing to her, *and* wondering where the hell he was taking her now, she stared out of the view screen, where the dot had reappeared on her retinas, this time burning a hole in the clear blue of a cloudless sky. An illusion, which lasted all of a second, when zip dirty, fraying curtains were slung on a line strung across it. Ditto: smog. This one had a sepia stink, which with the fishscale gloom, invaded the cabin with a briny tang. 'Goddam filters!' Julius snarled, 'Nano's supposed to keep that nasty shit out. You never know what's breeding down here.'

She turned to look at Fatberg, and the burning hole was back, framing his face, but when the cabin lights brightened, the edetic after-image, was gone, though never quite forgotten, for it was a strange moment, and one she would return to, when she first wondered what had possessed her to twine her life with his.

Was she crazy or what? Her impulsive 'yes' to the proposal – which she had wrung out of him (imagine!), sealed with a kiss before she ran into the bedroom and grabbed her ready to go bag from the wardrobe. On the roof, worrying if she'd locked the front door, which was ridiculous because no one but assassins ever called. Then, responding to Julius' urgent summons from above, scrambling up a yellow ladder towards a joke Pizza Hut, which was a seven-sided faux wood cylinder parked in the smog above her, like a fucking party hat. Yes, she'd actually sworn out loud, unforgivable, of course, but she'd been clutching her bag, hanging in the air below the open hatch, where Julius was standing, reaching down a hand, the red and green hazard flashing-lights around him lighting up the smog, like she was back in her teens, in a retro-disco in Rotorooa, New Zealand, when she'd first kissed a boy.

A minute later, the Pierspoint and her life in the apartment was gone, along with the spikes and spires of other tall buildings, and the spider lines of freeways intersecting the city as the Pizza Hut lifted above the smog and Julius set the cruising speed and directions. They had cocktails in the salon, where Julius chatted to the barbot, as the enormity of the change dawned on her.

Sometime later, in her new dressing room, she laid out four outfits on the bed from the rail of designer clothes in the wardrobe.

'Eeney Meeny Miney Mo,' she said, pointing in turn to the Persian Harlot, Tearaway Teen, Serious Secretary ...

Perhaps she really would be the Tsarina one day, she reconsidered. She imagined herself in the role as she stood looking at herself in the mirror of her suite of rooms in the most exclusive Pizza Hut in the world, adjusting the mohair brim of her stylish white hat she had picked out from an outfit in the ethnic rail in the wardrobe. Though the tiny print on the label, which had a little picture of a volcano on it, said it was made by the Warranka tribe in Peru, and the round brim wasn't strictly cowgirl, as soon as she saw it, she knew the hat was perfect.

But perfect to whom exactly? she thought. With the hat tipped at a racy angle, the eyes in the face studying her so intently from the mirror seemed to belong to a surreal self who might as well have been a character in a book for all she knew of her, because she was only halfway through reading chapter one of the story. Suddenly, she wanted to be that Carrie, that mysterious other self, which she suspected was as full of surprises as her Granmama's chest of fancy dressing-up clothes from before the Russian Revolution.

'Yes!' she murmured, sealing a secret compact with herself, 'out of the smog, make me the most perfectly surreal Tsarina ever!'

Wondering at her odd mood, half-regretting the wish, and feeling that the universe was shifting to accommodate the pent up feelings she had released with the impulse, she recalled Julius' caution as he'd ushered her from the ladder and into the hatch. He'd said that the containment field of the craft's propulsion drive affected people differently, but not to worry because any effect would soon settle down, though she might feel strange for a while.

A thoughtful expression on her face, she switched off the light in the closet and left the room, the silver heels of her dainty cowgirl boots, which complimented her mix-and-match outfit, clicking on the marble floor tiles as she turned left, towards the crew stairs (a misnomer – there was no crew, none being needed because everything was at the touch of a button, a voice or hand command) rather than the chrome doors of the elevator on the right, which ran up the outside and was basically a glass tube.

What Carrie didn't realize was that the odd interlude when she'd made her fateful wish had not, as she suspected, been brought on by the containment field of the craft's Imp-drive, but rather was the result of a thought string projected into her mind by another Jake, who was standing unseen right beside her at the time.

When Carrie slid open the crew hatch, and stepped down into the cabin, Fatberg was leaning over the retro instrument console, counting under his breath, as he often did when he thought no one was looking.

'Five hundred and twenty, four hundred and ten, three hundred and ninety-two point seven, one hundred and fifteen point two, seventy-five exactly, and ...' He looked up. 'Love the hat, very much, very too much, very, very, very you, moua moua miaow!' For good measure he blew her a kiss. 'Wait for it, wait for it, once again, Tsarina baby,' he chortled, chancing using the pet name he had picked for her – 'Once again, the captain of your heart makes a perfect landing,' he trumpeted.

The Pizza Hut settled down on its airbags, as hundreds, possibly thousands of pigeons disturbed by the sudden landing of the giant craft in the vast, empty square, flew up past the viewscreen.

'Where are we?' she said, disdaining to comment on his latest, stupidest, endearment yet. A cowgirl in a chair sat with one leg extended, and a cowgirl boot heel propped on the console before her, gazing out from under the brim of her new mohair hat at the ghostly outline of a great dome looming out of smog that seemed familiar somehow.

'Don't you recognize it?'

'For your sake I hope you've not brought us back in a circle?' she said, sitting up. But then her ready scowl was replaced by an expression of astonishment. As the swirling smog thinned a little, her jaw dropped, and she saw that the soaring dome did not, as she had first assumed, belong to a large, very controversial shopping mall a few miles from the apartment she had recently vacated, but instead was the dome and the two wings of the original edifice which the mall's profile exactly replicated – an ancient place of worship that was of supreme importance to a significant proportion of the population of the planet.

But rather less so for their iterations who, whether lucid or otherwise, rarely attach the same significance to objects as do their corporeal counterparts in the world of material existence, who whether believers or not, by dint of their physicality are inevitably so much more bound to place than are their other selves.

Iterations such as Jake2, who watched with amusement from his perch on a pink granite obelisk in the middle of the square, which at 25.12 m stood a mere .12 m higher than the Pizza Hut parked beside it. A metal ramp extended from the craft's lower deck and a little white bubble car, designed like a toy spaceship with wheels, just the passengers' heads showing under the perspex dome, one sitting straight-backed with the brim of her hat downturned. The other's head was bobbing, a hand gesticulating, as he drove down into the square around the obelisk, till he got a bearing, when he turned and proceeded in the direction of the great basilica.

A word here about the Pizza Hut's Imppulse drive.

He had already forgotten its dumb name, but the big number got Fatberg's attention after the hopeful had stood up and started his 5-minute pitch at the penultimate Invent-slam, events FakeReal had held in cities across the country back in the day, when the company was just a glorified start-up. Now, if he had understood right from the big guy in the spot, each second, the Universe manifested a total of 229,879,856,798,722,765.32 times.

Recognizing in the inventor a fellow counter, Fatberg then asked him,

'What do you do with all the numbers?'

'Null time,' the man, whose name Fatberg could never remember, (even though his squashed face with his car mats for eyebrows, and snarled black eyes that sometimes haunted him on the edge of sleep),

had said, 'that's where I put 'em. In the Drawer
of Infinite Depth, hidden in Null-space between
each one of them pulses. Skip a drawer, flip a
pulse, in the big M number, rich man,' (as, from
the start he had called Fatberg) 'and there you
have the impulse.'

Pointing to a dial on the portable Imp-
drive he had brought with him, he continued,

'Adjust the pulse with this, and the
seven phase containment field jumps any
which way. No energy required. Simple! It's
all done by dampening the oscillation of these
finely tuned titanium plates here, and upping
the oscillations on the other six plates to catch
the Null-energy surge, at the next non-
manifestation, when the pulse skips a beat
between Fibonacci sequences of the big M
number. Neat, huh? Up pulsing I call it,
though it really should be described as up-
down-side-pulsing, and compensating
interface energy displacement. The principal
being, rich man, move the field, and anything
you put in the field moves too.

Some small objects from the pockets of the panel were then moved in the air, in their respective confinement fields.

Questions followed.

Asked to expand on the operating principal, the inventor, said, 'Nothin' to it, rich man.' He shrugged. 'S'all 'bout switching push and resistance, between these here seven plates, which when scaled up can be embedded in any size of structure. While over here,' he said, reaching out a finger to sketch an invisible border about a foot from the small generator, which he said was approximated to the relative distance to size ratio of three over five, between the seven plates. 'Where the smaller containment field interfaces with the great universal one, which naturally is a whole lot bigger.'

It was at this point that the moderator intervened as, laughing at a joke no one else got, the inventor took out a chewed cheroot, which was later found to contain illegal substances, lit up, and released a great gust of smoke in which he was quickly removed by security, who were already in attendance (having been alerted by concerned members of the audience).

But he had said enough for Fatberg to be convinced. There was enough method in the madness, that when Fatberg caught up with the beat-up schmuck on the sidewalk outside, where security had tossed him a minute before, he offered his hand, before shaking on another fabulous FakeReal Associate deal.

This was despite the sucker's pitch being quite the worst in the invent-slam nationwide tour, which took in 17 identical conference centers in as many cities. It all soon blended into one dreary city, wrapping the country in as many tentacles, along which they sped as they avoided where possible convolutions, underpasses, and loop-overs, but less successfully the circumlocutions when posting to their fans – the hells angel outriders on their Harleys, clearing the traffic ahead of the speeding motorcade of limos, which one chat-host called:

'This righteous cavalcade of privileged billionaire brats of the new perp industry in their e-chariots, on a mission to replace manifest reality with fake dreams, turn you and me into avatars, rob our kids of a future, poison us with interactive porn, and steal the world from under our feet.'

With the widely publicized invent-slams, which soon went viral, viewers debated maths versus common sense, questioned shopping and argued whether the earth was a shrink-wrapped pizza hologram or a Monsters of the Panty-Verse computer game. The new Corporation scraped up the raw talent universities across the land had cast aside and wrapped them up in FakeReal Associate deals they could never get out from, until they were fired.

Turned out, the Imp-drive was everything the Inventor claimed. However, it was canned shortly before going into production, after the Pentagon deemed that the new Imp-Tech was too disruptive, except for them, which didn't come as a surprise to Fatberg. Anticipating just such a turn, he had already snaffled the only prototypes, M-1, M-2, and M-3.

Too bad the inventor couldn't handle his generous compensation package from the government agency who took over the defense contract under clause 402 of the Strategic Industries Requisition Provisions: Emergency Powers Act, Sub-section C. He was last heard of in a small town on Highway 41, down in the former Everglades. The investigator assigned to his case, reported the subject was in the business of farming 'gators and wasn't doing well, with the drought, no mud for wallowing his dehydrated 'gators, and his increasing consumption of methamphetamine; he was acting out the sad decline of a near genius. Still couldn't remember the man's name. Call him Inventor FR Associate 201. Most likely dead by now, if not from the drugs then from his pet 'gators, which the investigator said wandered freely about the boat house beached in the dried-up lake down in the Never Glades, as the news shows called them now. Shame, Fatberg might have dropped in on him and compared notes about the counting, but now it was too late.

At long last, Fatberg understood his compulsion was, and had always been, about figuring out what the hell the universe would manifest next. Each moment ended in a cliff-hanger, with a null gap you could fall into, before the next moment.

He was never so scared of them as then, as a small child, standing at the bottom of a long flight of stairs, determined to climb the steps on his own. He'd had to figure out the how and where to place his feet. First, his outside leg, making sure his big toe was all the way in, then made his inside leg push up (which was nearest the wall) and lifted his foot over the gap onto the next step. Determined, the jaw proud, his tiny teeth clamped in grim concentration, careful not make a sound, not looking down at his feet in case he put them off and he fell in a gap. One by one, he mounted the risers, the counting the easy part, because he could already count up to fifty-five in just three breaths. Worst was crossing the gaps which he felt reaching up to grab him through the soles of his feet, petrified each time. Looking up, he saw that the red hand of the big round clock above, at the head of the stairs, was counting his steps as it swept round the dial. His foot stopped, it stopped, he moved a fraction, and it moved, also a fraction, like they were playing a game ...

But then the moment was gone, when he heard his father calling him from the garden, where the sun was shining, the light spilling in through the open front door, his father's long shadow stretching an arm and a pointing black finger to where yellow sunlight lapped the gleaming wooden boards at the bottom of the stairs...

*

THE GREAT OLYMPUS GAMES –
SCENE #3 EPISODE 23

'SILENCE!

'But I …'

'SILENCE I SAID,' Zeus thundered. 'The prisoner has had ample opportunity to respond to the charges. We have heard enough evidence,'

'This is ridiculous,' Prometheuz yelled, his blood rushing to his head all of a sudden, his earbud buzzing as he veered off-script in his first line of dialogue. 'I haven't heard anything. Just what am I charged with? I only just got here!

'HEY!' he cried, jumping back as a sizzling bolt of white fire struck the stone dock, which though non-fungible, felt real enough when he withdrew his scorched fingertips from the seared line on the cheap prop conforming to the outline of the dock, where he had gripped the 3D printed rail. There was a disparity between fungible and non-fungible furniture, sight and touch, combined with the drag of his cumbersome heavy new muscles, as Zeus in his high chair glowered down at him, the biggest fake of all. He felt he had been suckered against his will into the part, not even being told he was playing a prisoner, the dupe of one and all including billions of livestreaming perps. All he wanted to be locked in his cell, safe behind a steel door, with the double blind world, and all in it, shut out.

'SILENCE!' Zeus raised a lightning rod finger. 'OR I WILL STRIKE YOU DOWN.'

'Almighty Father.' Dionysus stepped out and stood, hands clasped humbly before him, craftily looking up under dipped eyelids at Zeus. The Father was leaning out from his high chair above the steep, worn steps cut in the gigantic, clear crystal boulder, jazzed with veins of gold, which supported the almighty father's great throne.

'If I may be allowed to intercede.'

'SPEAK!'

'What I have to say is not for lesser

gods to hear, oh Almighty Father.'

'VERY WELL THEN,' Zeus rumbled, directing a spark at the steps, which lit up. 'APPROACH.'

Taking the opportunity of the first moment he was not the center of the attention, Prometheuz carefully scanned his surroundings. In the foreground, ranged in concentric half circles facing him, were rows of benches divided by an aisle. On the left side, Poseidon sat impassively, while two demigods of the Prosecution debated across him. Across the aisle, however, the first and second row of the benches reserved for the Defense were empty, which figured, Prometheuz thought.

Further back, both sides of the aisle, benches were filling up with gods and their acolytes. Middle of one group, tall Athena unmistakable under a red-crested golden motorcycle helmet, her famous AK 74 automatic assault rifle, which supposedly was solid platinum and 100% real, gripped in her mighty left hand, and the owl that sees everything perched on her broad right shoulder. At the back, between the benches and the ring of non-fungible pillars, ushers walked about in their birthday suits or body suits, either way ridiculous, beaming as they welcomed more gods and their entourages into the vast Hall of Zeus every few seconds.

Each time was heralded by a brilliant flash – red, gold. Hermes was the only god who arrived alone, while Ares made the biggest entrance. Announced by a dark red flash, he blazed in, dressed like a cowboy, except for the horns that poked out of his big Stetson hat. One hand was raised in salute as he stood astride the hood of a bonnet of a red corvette with whitewall tyres and twin mufflers jetting flames, like he was descending on a flying chariot, as might be expected of the God of War.

The illusion of a crowded concourse held all the way to the pillars. Projected in blacklight between them were the invisible, blacklight field distortion lenses, which the make-up girl had said were multi-directional, which he took to mean two-way and brought everything right up close, no matter where you were standing. And it was true; when his gaze lingered on any of the perps shuffling in the outer darkness beyond, their monstrous faces and the eyes on him enlarged, until the hairy warts became hillocks, and their scars crevasses, giving him the feeling he was a hamster in a cage surrounded by ravenous monsters.

None was more grotesque than Medusa. When he picked her out among the perps and focussed on her, she swelled in size until she filled the space between non-fungible pillars. She had a basket of snakes for a head, which fortunately was turned away, otherwise he might have been turned to stone, or so the legend went in his Grandfather's book of Ancient Greek Myths, he suddenly recalled, taking that to be a hopeful sign the elusive story would pop into his mind.

Of course, he knew the monsters ranging the tiers of the make-believe amphitheater beyond the pillars were only avatars. Some, he realized, could be friends, nursing resentments at his elevation to godhood status, joining in the baying mob livestreaming on the Home Pay-2-Perp Service. He hoped not, for their sakes, whenever they came to their senses, in some far-off future when the smog lifted, the Emergency restrictions ended, and the world was not shut-down. For himself, his mind kept shying away from whatever the fuck was coming round the next corner. Just dealing with what was before him was enough.

Seeking distraction, he looked up at the distant dome, which had been likened to a sieve in the chat boxes. Much significance was given to the fact there were 33 windows piercing it, and to their cunning mandala arrangement. From the non-fungible universe beyond into the dome, through the angular little windows, blacklight poured in arabesque isosceles veils, in full glorious holo-vision that consistently got a max 5 on the EyeCandy rating on the V-Travel Trust Guide, and had been compared to the Igazu Falls in South America as they had appeared before they generated electricity.

So those were the heavens. On the set, groups of conspicuously-muscled male gods and equally voluptuous female gods comingled, in pools of blacklight that shafted down from above. Each god glowed, radiating a signature colour – blue, green, gold, red, purple – and every shade in between. Unmistakable, among their entourages of acolytes, hangers on, demigods, and such. Each face a living sculpture, majestic, every kind of twisted, morose, indifferent and beautiful in the same moment, each god having a different portion of each. Lyre birds chirped on their shoulders, shoals of fish swam in the air about them, marking an absence of sea.

Actually, Prometheuz didn't think hardly any of this, or see the fish, though he later thought he had. Instead, apart from the rating on Trust Guide™, the thought string had been beamed into the medulla oblongata of his brain by his iteration - who had been with him all the way from the muscle clinic and, unseen, was perched on the dock at

Prometheuz's elbow, kicking his heels, watching everything and reading the lines no one else saw, converging on the set from billions on HM -BDY, Pay-2-Perp, and all the other livestreaming channels.

*

THE GREAT OLYMPUS GAMES –
SCENE #4 EPISODE 23

'SILENCE IN COURT,' Zeus thundered, bolts of lightning flashing from the non-fungible dark clouds roiling about his great head.

'SILENCE!' he repeated. His great eyes searched the Gods' faces in the hall below for sarcastic expressions and other signs of dissent as they looked back up at him. 'GOOD!' he rumbled, 'I have been informed by... ah...' He frowned, looked down.

'Dionysus, Almighty Father,' Dionysus grinned lopsidedly, 'Your fifth son.'

'Really?' Zeus raised an eyebrow that resembled a thornbush.

'Mnemosyne will help you recall which one I am. She is near, I can summon her, Almighty Father.'

'I need no assistance from the daughter of the Muse to recall your miserable hide, Dionysus, nor the way you took to the wine cup even before you were weaned. Bah! You were a drunkard when a godling, and now you stand before me, in your red cloak of a public defender, still a drunkard, representing another reprobate.' Zeus nodded towards Jake in the dock, before adding in a foghorn boom, for the benefit of anyone in the court not paying attention, 'THE PRISONER.'

'Who, I must point out, has lately been deserted by Mnemosyne and so remembers nothing of the proceedings thus far,' Dionysus interjected, hastily. 'And has not been found guilty for the crimes, Almighty Father.' He offered up his trademark grin. 'Yet!' he added.

'Indeed, I take your point.' Zeus nodded. 'Even though I never heard a more open and shut case.'

'Almighty Father, even you ...' Dionysus pleaded from the steps below.

'Yes I know,' Zeus sighed, heavily. Pointing to a nearby stone column and its inscription, he read out. 'Law Two: no god will be condemned without a fair hearing before his peers. And listen to Law Four. All gods are equal before the Law. I must have been under the influence of Eros when I carved that.' He chortled into his beard. Though restrained, his laughter shook the pillars of the Great Hall, alarming the gods gathered below, who all knew all too well the destruction that often followed Zeus's mirth.

'Almighty Father,' Dionysus pleaded, more forcefully. 'He is the youngest Titan of your generation. Your cousin!'

'Indeed. And long has he troubled me.'

'If not for him, surely for his father and the immortal ichor churning in our veins, Almighty Father,' Dionysus pleaded, hopefully.

'You dare invoke Cronus, my father.' Zeus thundered, still feeling guilty over castrating his father, though not over murdering him.

'I would not dare so to presume.' Dionysus hung his head, looked back at Prometheuz, and winked.

'Hmm,' Zeus rumbled. 'Very well, I will

grant your request, since there is nothing to the contrary to suggest that the, um ...'

'The accused,' Dionysus prompted.

The mighty brow of Zeus furrowed as if Circe had just harrowed it with her plough. Leaning over the arm of his throne, he glared down at Dionysus, who rapidly shrank under the power of his gaze till he was no bigger than a pea, but then rebounded to his usual size.

After a meaningful pause intended to communicate to Dionysus the narrowness of his escape, Zeus continued, 'In consideration of the claims put forwards by my fifth son, his reprobate defender, that Mnemosyne for reasons known only to her sweet immortal self has lately deserted the prisoner, and taken his memory of the proceedings, I rule that his confessions shall be replayed so that he might benefit from witnessing from his own mouth the full account he gave to all gathered here of his crimes.'

*

CHAPTER 5

DBUKSET Channel WKYTUBE: intercept conversation on FakeNet between Dmbwtz and Scoop-a-Perp. Analysis: 72.4-82.8% poss. C.R. P.–

D. I say it's an authentic apparition.

SP. I'm not so sure, the freeze-holo is not at all clear.

D. Five of the six hex-cams follow it as it drops from the dock and walks towards P. on the benches ...

SP. Who doesn't see it, even though he's looking straight at it.

D. Obviously it's invisible to the actors, even Prom, who's closest most of the time.

SP. Could be a hack attack by a rival corporation, like that one years back, in that otherwise totally forgettable FauxReel show, Bo-Peep.

D. I will never forget that. My kids were livestreaming episode five when those demon avatars broke through the V-thing. Fucking wrecked the living room.

SP. How is that possible?

D. At first, I didn't believe it either. But the damage was so extensive. Like a cyclone had passed through. I found my kids quaking under the sofa, where it had been tossed in a corner with the rest of the busted furniture.

SP. You serious?

D. Absolutely, the kids were totally traumatized.

SP. You could have sued.

D. Oh, I contemplated it, to be sure. I V-cammed everything, and for back-up took photos, then got a neighbor to witness the damage. But in the end I decided against.

SP. Why?

D. Well, what finally put me off was the thought of my kids having to relive the trauma every time the case came to court.

SP. Every time?

D. Just supposing we won the first time, with all those lawyers FuxReel keep on the books, it was bound to be appealed to a higher court, and so on, right to the top.

SP. The Supreme Court?

D. Sure, if we got that far.

SP. Might be interesting. Think about it, by the time you got there, you'd be a fully qualified lawyer.

D. You know, I think that's 'bout the most intelligent thing I have ever heard you say.

SP. Why thank you.

D. Seriously, I mean it. But what put me off in the end was imagining my boys being cross-examined under auto-stim, by some dick-brain prof, who can pull out of my boys' minds just anything they want.

SP. They can do that?

D. Uh-huh. I read up on some cases in the court records. One guy who sued FauxReel for messing up his kids' heads ended up convicted of molesting them. Next his wife divorced him, and now he's down in the subs. Happens all the time.

SP. Yea, up one rung, then woops, down a slippery v-snake.

D. I didn't mean it literally.

SP. Hey, you're supposed to be the dumb one.

D. Yes, but switching roles is fun, as you know because you done it before.

SP. Done what? You messing with my head again?

D. Was not aware you had one.

SP. Doh!

*

Turning away as Julius continued jabbering at her, Carrie noticed that the obelisk, which had been to her right a moment before, was now to the left of the little bubble car.

Seen though the dripping perspex bubble, it resembled a giant upright needle, balanced in the smog, seeming to draw etheric phantoms from all around. The eye, where she supposed the base of the column to be, was threaded by a long, spooling line that was tied to the bobbin of the bubble car in which she was trapped with Julius. He was supposed to know where he was going since he was the CEO of the biggest corporation on the planet, with a T/O greater than the combined member nations of the EU, but obviously he was lost for directions.

She didn't have a clue either. The one and only living claimant to the throne of Russia. Herself, she thought, Ms Caroline Emilia Anastasia Romanov aka Erheart, lately of apartment 223 in the Pierspoint Building.

Zip …? She couldn't now remember. Because none of that existed now, only the smog which had stolen the world, and Jake, from her. She wondered if he was better off down in the subs, away from her nagging, which he was always complaining of …

'Why the long sigh?' Julius suddenly said, breaking into her thoughts.

Carrie turned away from her window, then started with fright as a pack bot, in green and gold livery, its pannier piled with packages, loomed in the windshield.

'Watch out!' she yelped, as the bubble car somehow missed it. 'You might have hit the poor thing.'

'Not a chance,' Julius laughed, 'they've got AVT.'

'What's that?'

'Avoidance V-tech, you couldn't run one over if you tried. He's a clever bastard.'

'Who?'

'My closest competitor. Montague-Evans.'

When she gave him a blank look, he added, sneeringly, 'The Bot King, so-called. Ugly things aren't they?'

'They're everywhere, and more so since the universal shut-in.' Carrie said, as she peered into the smog to see where it went, noticing that the obelisk had disappeared and had been replaced by the faint outline of the dome.

'Aren't you going to ask me who's expecting us?'

'The Pope, who else?'

'How'd you guess?'

'Well, you being who you are, us on our way to get married, and that being the Vatican.' She pointed at the dome, which had added colonnades to the left and right sides, and a whole lot of statues besides, since she last looked. 'If my new fantasy life with you was a story in a book, most readers would have already worked that out.'

'Remarkable,' Julius muttered with a little shake of his head as he peered into the smog.

'Tell me, how much did it cost?'

'I'm not sure I quite understand.' Julius frowned.

'Donate, as in build a new cathedral, fund cancer research, send missionaries to the moon,' she laughed. 'What do I know?'

'Oh, I see what you mean,' he said, flashing a disingenuous smile. 'I always leave that to others who are more expert in such matters.'

'So modest!' She grinned.

'Look.' He pointed ahead, over the steering wheel. 'I do believe that is our escort party. Do you see there, coming down those steps?'

'Yes. Not so sure about the face masks, though.' She smiled again at the incongruity, with their steel helmets, breastplates, scarlet hosiery, and the antiquated pointed halberds held by the Swiss Guards, marching two abreast down the steps, as the bubble car drew to a stop below.

Watching the scene from his perch on top of the obelisk, Jake2 smiled to himself.

Now the long spooling line was following the pair up the steps, and through a door into the great Basilica beyond. It was a very obedient line.

*

THE GREAT OLYMPUS GAMES –
EPISODE 23 SCENE#5

Prometheuz prised apart an encrusted eyelid with a grimy fingernail, just enough for a splinter of light to irradiate his brain and induce a humungous headache. Bad mistake.

His next mistake was attempting to stand up. The fact he couldn't have done it without the support of a tree did not take away from his sense of achievement as he urinated against it, fortunately without splashing his bare legs too much. At last he risked opening one eye wide enough to make out blurred foliage, stunted trees, and knotty faces leering back at him from gnarled, convoluted boughs and dipping branches. Oh fuck, the party.

Now he remembered Dionysus prancing ahead on his cloven hooves, leading him into a woodland glade towards a ring of drunken satyrs, and gyrating nymphs dancing around a blazing fire, sparks spiraling towards a billion twinkling stars in the clear night sky.

But where the hell was he? More to the point who was he? Oh yea, he remembered, a grossly muscled god with a god-sized hangover. He laughed, and immediately regretted it, feeling at any second his head might disengage from his spine and roll off his shoulders. The tree helped as he slid on his back down its trunk and slumped onto something hard, which lodged in the cleft of his naked buttocks. It was an acorn, he discovered, as once again he settled back onto the damp patch between gnarled tree roots.

So, the stunted trees were ancient oaks – unless of course the trees were non-fungible, he considered as he flicked the acorn away. However, the trunk at his back seemed solid enough.

Uh, it was starting to coming back to him. Dionysus pleading his case in Court, Zeus up in his high chair, Poseidon glaring from the benches of the gods of the Prosecution, perps cruising in the darkness beyond the ring of pillars. Then, after Zeus adjourned the proceedings, and as Prometheuz had been following Dionysus out of the court, he noticed him retrieving the blob from the back of the bench where he'd stuck it. Next thing, the pillars of the great hall had disappeared, and the god was leading him into a clearing in a wood, passing him a bulging wine skin filled with cheap plonk, urging him to drink up and promising him a night such as he would never forget in the long days and nights to come of the next ten thousand years.

He'd balked at that, taking the statement to indicate the god expected a guilty verdict when they returned to court. But instead of denying it, Dionysus produced the blob from his shirt pocket, and before he could stop him promptly pressed it to his ear.

Immediately, over the sounds of revelry from around the fire, he heard Poseidon's unmistakable baritone.

'The delay will not change anything. Zeus will see through all Dionysus' tricks. Prometheuz has had this coming a long time. But I'll only be satisfied when I hear Zeus deliver the maximum sentence.

'Don't worry, Bro,' Dionysus said, reaching out and picking the blob from Prometheuz's ear. 'Poseidon's always absurdly confident until things go against him, which they always do in the end, as when he lost the contest for the sky, which Zeus won of course.' Dionysus looked down at the blob in his open hand. 'There will be a lot more audio on this, some of which will give us the edge when we return to court.' He grinned lopsidedly, then slapped Prometheuz on the back, heartily. 'Drink up, Bro, but don't get too incapable.' He winked, meaningfully.

How could he forget Aphrodite descending into the clearing in a shower of gold dust. Completely naked, of course, since being the most beautiful god of all she had nothing to hide and she never wore a scrap of clothes.

Despite heeding Dionysus' caution, Prometheuz had ended up beating his detumenising dick against the trunk of a gnarled oak, which turned out to be a cheap prop like just about everything else in this dumb reality he'd somehow stumbled into. Drunk, he'd completely forgotten the oak grove was a v-set and billions were livestreaming his performance.

It started off well enough when they grappled, as gods generally do when engaging in foreplay, but then, as he mounted Aphrodite's golden clam and saddled up, hearing loud hooting, he'd glanced round and saw a ring of the perps peeping into the grove, their ogling eyes gleaming in the darkness beyond. Result, instant shriveled dick. But goaded by her golden whip, he renewed his assault, but from a new angle, enduring more lashes and a lot of scorn before he breached and, as they say on Mount Olympus, *god down on her*. His head squeezed between her immortal thighs, he knew despair, but bravely kept grinding on with the stubble on his genoplast-enhanced chin, and the other tools available to him, until she came like a semi-automatic – and he was almost decapitated by her scissor legs.

Then, after she left without a backwards look, in a great huff of golden sparks, Prometheuz stomped about the grove looking around every tree for his trousers. Had the perps run off with them, he wondered, by that time having completely forgotten he was only an actor in a v-production.

*

'Here he comes.' Julius nudged Carrie, as they waited in the Sacristy, where the Swiss Guards had left them in the charge of a tall, taciturn, heavily built priest, who Julius guessed was papal security.

'Oh god,' Carrie muttered to herself, wishing she was wearing a less outlandish outfit than her mix-and match ensemble, she'd picked out from her clothes closet.

Appropriately, as will be explained, the Pope's imminence was announced by the sound of rapidly approaching footsteps.

Unusually, since he was still very much alive, 82-year-old Gregorius XVIII was already considered by Church historians to be one of the greatest reforming popes. However, despite his achievement in reuniting the mother church with the Orthodox Greek and Russian churches which had broken away in

1054, in the 'Great Schism', he was popularly known as the *Walking Pope.*

'My dears,' said the energetic old man in his simple white robes, with his twinkling blue eyes. He held out both hands as he walked towards them, the heels of his famous red shoes clicking on the marble floor.

Behind him came his secretary, a thin, sallow-faced wiry man with beady black eyes behind gold-framed round spectacles, wearing a conservative black suit, patent leather lace-up shoes, and carrying a clipboard in one hand and a gold fountain pen in his other. Behind him, struggling to keep up, came two fat, perspiring priests in black cassocks, who clearly were not used to exercise.

'Ho un matrimonio da officiare. Vai ora, dì alle guardie di essere nella cappella, quando arriviamo lì.' the Pontiff said, with a nod at the two fat priests, who were both obviously relieved to be dismissed, and scuttled away.

'My dear Ms Erheart.' He beamed beatifically as she curtseyed – something she had never done before, but felt impelled to do. 'Or perhaps I should say, Ms Romanov.' He raised an eyebrow, their eyes meeting as she stood up.

'How?' she blurted, totally astonished that he knew her real name.

'My dear,' he said, lightly taking Carrie's hand in his fingers, 'a source of great sorrow to my predecessors, and of course my fellow Patriarchs in our united church, is the terrible tragedy suffered by your family. You have always been in our prayers.'

Half-turning, he extended his other hand. 'Welcome, my dear Julius,' he said. 'Without your great generosity, and the Holy Channels our good friends in FauxReel have provided during this awful Emergency, in one hundred and forty-seven languages no less, the sufferings of the United Church would have been immeasurably greater!'

'It has been our privilege, and a personal honor, Holy Father,' Julius mumbled, uncharacteristically, his head bowed.

'This is such a happy day!' the Pope exclaimed. 'Come, let us walk together. Isn't it wonderful we have the whole of the Vatican to ourselves.'

Walking between them, hand in hand, he led them down a long barrel-vaulted corridor, with Ancient Roman statues at intervals in niches along the walls.

Behind them, scribbling down everything the Pope said, trotted the secretary, who in turn was followed by the taciturn priest.

'I have a confession to make,' the Pope said, in a different tone. 'Since the Emergency began, I have found myself, shall we say, appreciating certain, um, aspects of the restrictions we are all under.'

'Really, Holy Father?' Carrie, who was enjoying her first real exercise (apart from on her treadmill) in three long years, asked.

'Yes, my dear,' he said, 'I am afraid it is true. You are aware what many people call me?'

'The Walking Pope?'

'Yes my dear,' he nodded pontifically, slowing his pace slightly for the benefit of Julius, who though fit, and never shut-in like 99% of the population these past 3 years, had started panting. 'And until recently, never was a name less deserved.'

'How is that, Holy Father?' Carrie asked, politely.

'Well, my dear, ever since I entered the Church, I have always been the *walking* something or other. First I was called the Walking Novice, and later the Walking *Priest*. Life was simple then, there were no limousine drivers to become unemployed if I didn't permit them to take me everywhere. With every elevation the walking became more difficult, as more obstacles were placed in my way. As a Bishop in Africa I had to exercise my ecclesiastical powers just to be permitted to walk the last few miles to any village or town I visited in the course of my duties, and even then I had to walk at the pace of the slowest of my entourage.

'My ambulatory difficulties were only compounded when I was appointed a cardinal, and of course by then the entourage had considerably swelled in size. I didn't think things could possibly get any worse, until, for my sins, my fellow cardinals plotted to make me pontiff, and unfortunately, after several recounts, succeeded!' He laughed. 'My favourite TV serial on the very limited choices we had then on Vatican Cable became *The Prisoner*, perhaps because, cut off as I found myself in the papal apartments, I soon identified with the protagonist. But then that was a decade ago, before this, um…'

The Pope lowered his voice, so his secretary, taking notes a discrete five paces behind, could not hear. 'The *blessed* Emergency came along,' he laughed, 'and I discovered that to my great joy I could make a complete circuit of these buildings, which according to the pedometer on my leg is twenty-two point two two kilometers, and without ever once stepping outside.'

They had reached the end of the long corridor of statues. 'Now,' the Pope smiled, 'I must stop talking as before us, we have one of the great wonders of Christendom, which also I believe has been inspirational for our friends at FauxReel with their new popular V-show.'

'Please don't repeat that to others, Holy Father,' Julius interjected.

'Why, my son?' the Pope, asked, stopping in the entrance of the Sistine Chapel.

'My critics would use it against me, Holy Father, and, um, I don't think it would go down too well with our core audience if they learned we modelled Zeus on the image Michelangelo painted of Almighty God.' Julius pointed up at the ceiling. 'And all the other elements we borrowed, with your permission, of course, Holy Father,' he added, hastily.

'Well, that was entertainment for the masses then, I suppose,' the Pontiff sighed. 'It was a very different world when Michelangelo painted his murals.'

Both Julius and Carrie had only wanted a simple wedding. So they got a simple pastor to bless them – the Pope! Well, Julius was who he was. Besides, he was owed a favor or two for the lifeline FauxReel had extended to the Mother Church since the start of Emergency.

The place was the Sistine Chapel under the famous mural of the story of Genesis. On the wall before them loomed Michelangelo's other great mural, The Last Judgement. One giant figure in particular kept drawing Carrie's attention. Crouched with one hand over an eye, he had an expression of utmost horror on his face, as two devils dragged him by the legs down to the fires of hell. Something about him reminded her of Jake, not so much his physique, though there were similarities, nor his anguished expression, but most definitely his uncovered eye – which she felt watched her intently throughout.

The ceremony was just as they wanted – short and simple. All that was required from the Pope were the words, 'Ti pronuncio uomo e moglie,' which his secretary wrote on a lined page on his clipboard. The Pope added his initials below, then one of the Swiss Guards standing by was summoned to sign his name, and it was done – they were married!

Bi-located in the giant's eye on the wall mural, Jake2 was curious about the movements of the v-cams, all of which had been tracking the happy couple ever since they entered the chapel.

The marriage ceremony was of no interest him, other than that it was the direct result of his manipulations and as such entirely satisfactory. From the lines which enmesh the world, that intersected the space, he should have been able to determine who or what was viewing the happy couple, but after he identified the one line out of all those intersecting the space, whenever he attempted to trace the line back to its source, a dangerous elemental which he perceived as a giant snake blocked him – a snake that looked suspiciously like the one tempting Eve, in the ceiling panel ...

*

Feeling his head could explode at any moment, Prometheuz closed his eyes. But he couldn't shut out the images of himself which Mnemosyne, who was supposed to be his sister, projected in the air before him.

Himself, if he was to believe his eyes, shaping the evil manikins from clay, then breathing life into them.

'That alone merited banishment from Olympus,' Poseidon thundered, levelling his trident accusingly at him.

But worse, the clay was mixed with dirt, which the imposter had secretly collected from the Proving Grounds where the Gods settled disputes, upon which, over the ages, had been spilt much immortal ichor – blood, he was supposed to understand.

Again, he had been unable to deny the evidence presented before him in holographic detail.

That immortal blood, and his breath, had bestowed on the perps consciousness, an attribute which was the property of the gods alone. But the worst crime had been to steal fire from Zeus's hearth and give it to the perps, along with the secrets of writing, numbers, and artifice. Now fires raged across Gaia, the playground planet that Zeus had constructed for the pleasure of the Gods and its resident spirits – all the different kinds of nymphs, nereids, satyrs, dryads, panes and tritons that looked after its precious mountains, pastures, forests, wetlands, pools lakes, springs, streams, rivers, seas and oceans, and the habitats of its many species of creatures. But not satisfied wreaking destruction across what had been the loveliest of planets in all of Creation, now the perps were plotting to storm heaven and overthrow Olympus.

'Do you still deny your crimes, perp lover!' Poseidon demanded, brandishing his trident.

'Yes, absolutely!' Prometheuz stubbornly insisted. 'All the evidence has been faked. None of this is down to me. Heaven knows I hate the perps as much as the next god! Ever since I was a little Titan I ...'

'I have heard enough!' Zeus thundered, cutting off Prometheuz mid-peroration. 'Despite all his denials, the Prisoner is clearly guilty, of all the charges.'

He glared down at Prometheuz. 'Have you anything to say in mitigation before I pronounce sentence?'

'This is a set up!' Prometheuz protested. 'I've been framed.'

'Silence, prisoner.' Zeus raised a hand threateningly.

'Oh go and fuck yourself, Almighty Father. I've had enough of this shit.'

As the perspicacious reader may already have noted, Jake had become so absorbed in his role he had begun to believe he really was Prometheuz.

This is a danger of the technique of method acting, particularly for amateur thespians who can fail to recognize when they have reached the point of no return, beyond which there is no way back to who they were when they started playing the part.

*

CHAPTER 6

Conversation on the FauxReel Culture Vultures Channel: 235:hrs. 13/10/43.

'We've had all this before!'

'Not so, Petronella. If you think back, they have reprised it with some very significant differences.'

'You mean *slightly* different, which you know well, Elliot, amounts to much the same. Really, it's an outrage!'

'Perhaps you're exaggerating a little, Petronella.'

'The cheek! I could peck the eyes out of the chicken brain genius who dreamed-up this cheap wheeze, really I could. How much do the poo pellet counters upstairs fucking save? I'm so disappointed, Elliot. And to cap it off, I discover that this goddamn vulture avatar can't cry. If you could see me now in my v-tent, Elliot.'

'Hush, Petronella, we don't talk of that, remember. Look on the bright side, I think it's a plot curve.'

'What do you mean? Preposterous! Plots need to keep to the point, not stray and go curvy. Really!'

'Think of it, Petronella, this might be the most vital twist, when the trajectory goes bendy. A T-bendy they call it. *(looks down)* I think. Not sure about the 'y' though.'

'And tonight you, Elliot, bandy bendy words about rather more than usual!'

'If you'd listen, instead of squawking so loudly, you might hear ...'

'What?

'Well ...' *(pause)*

'You were going to say *(yawn)* to expect a great scene.'

'No ... I mean, uh, yes, *absolutely*, Petronella! The more disappointment you feel now, the greater will be your surprise when ...'

'When what, Elliot? What am I to expect?' *(fluffs breast feathers)*

'Gore, Petronella, gore. I predict there will be so much gore, as never before. Enough even to satisfy you *(laughs)*, my dear. Or perhaps I will turn everyone to stone, trigger a monster quake on Mount Olympus and bring down the non-fungible pillars of Zeus' temple with a full-on stare of my three hundred and thirty-three pairs of snake eyes *(Shakes head – Medusa snakes wiggle)*. What do you think!? *(superior smile)*

'My tally app counts six hundred and sixty-six snake eyes *(peers at each pair in turn)*. Which ones are yours, Elliot?'

'You are entering dangerous territory *(note of venom)*. Take care, Petronella.'

'What? You worried that I might guess?' *(sinister titter)*

'We all have our secrets, Petronella. I always respect yours.'

'Oh ho! I didn't see much evidence of that when you crossed the set and were an item with Gerald in the Basilisk Pen.'

'Now, you know we don't give other's names. Remember, rules of the game. The privacy of the perp is always paramount. That's basic, Petronella. Basic! And never you forget it.' *(snake hisses)*

'How I wish I could *(pronounced squawk)*, every time you remind me.'

*

Dazed after the rushed preparations for the next scene, in which he was alternatively pummeled, told to sit up, lie down, had his head put in restraints, was turned over, scrubbed, force-fed liquids by tube and enemas, his mind was as empty of thought as the chassis of a car shunting along a factory assembly line. Only in his case it wasn't robots installing parts, but cosmeticians, masseurs, chiropractors, dental technicians, and other specialists working him over. All the while his voice coach walking alongside, making him repeat the lines she recited again and again.

As has already been noted, confused as to who he was at the start of the process, by the time they were through with him in the body shop located below the set, his old self was as distant to him as the young child is to the adult. To be sure, in a corner of his mind, the old Jake was still there, but out of reach of is manufactured new self. This 'immortal' creature of enhanced genoplast ever-renewing flesh, this sacrificial victim with such exaggerated musculature was finally ready for all those monstrous perps cruising in the darkness, beyond the set.

'Cooeee!

Fatberg groaned, as he recognized the familiar voice. 'Speak of the devil,' he said in a resigned tone, regretting having accepted the call from the CEO of Styx2U on his private v-number.

'First sign of madness!

'What do you mean?' Fatberg scowled back at the cocky homunculus in a green suit with its gold lapels. He was standing hands on hips on the little pedestal, where he had just manifested next to Fatbcrg's elbow.

'Well, I don't see anyone else in the cabin with you,' the little man said, archly, pointedly looking about.

'Oh I see,' Fatberg sniffed. 'Your name came up earlier in conversation, that's all. What do you want, Montague? I'm busy right now.'

'Actually, I called to congratulate you!'

'About what?' Fatberg's eyes narrowed.

'Oh I see,' Fatberg sniffed. 'Your name came up earlier in conversation, that's all. What do you want, Montague? I'm busy right now.'

'Actually, I called to congratulate you!'

'About what?' Fatberg's eyes narrowed.

'On getting married, dear chap. Had I known earlier I would have sent you a big bunch of something smelly. It's about time! Ha. And your mystery new wife did look lovely in that extraordinary –'

'How did you find out?' Fatberg snapped.

'On FauxReel, where else? It's all over the v-waves.'

'I wonder, who was the source?' Fatberg said pointedly.

'Not me, old boy, you have to look elsewhere for that. Lots of speculation about your lovely new wife by the way. You would have thought nothing else had happened in the world today. I must say, dear chap, it really was a coup getting the Pope to do the honors.'

'Goodbye, Montague!' Fatberg said, firmly, peremptorily ending the v-call just as Carrie, her hair still damp after taking a shower, entered the little cabin. She was wearing a Japanese kimono she'd discovered among the designer outfits in her voluminous clothes closet.

'Who was that?' she asked, settling into the other chair.

'Nobody!' he said. Then, when she raised an enquiring eyebrow, he added with a calculated shrug, 'You know, business.'

'Poor Julius.' She patted his arm, 'No escape even on our honeymoon.'

'Did you have a nice nap?'

'Hmm, yes. I feel so refreshed,' she smiled, 'and all the better because in the rush to leave the apartment I forgot my handheld.'

'You did?' Fatberg could barely disguise his relief.

She nodded. 'Where are we flying over now?'

'Ah let me see.' Julius peered at his instrument panel. 'Yes, as of now DD four two, point four-nine nine-nine eight.'

'Julius, you should know by now, all those figures mean nothing to me. I need a name.'

'Ok.' Julius typed the numbers on a pad. 'Ah, apparently we are directly over the highest point in the Caucasus Mountain range, which is eighteen thousand six hundred and –'

'Julius!' Carrie snapped, 'What did I just say?'

*

CHAPTER 7

THE GREATEST OLYMPUS GAMES –
EPISODE 23 SCENE#6

(Banner Headline Emblazoned Across the Sky)

'DAY 1 – THE NEXT 100,000 YEARS'

From afar, it was a gash on the face of a blasted mountain-top.

Closer to, however, the gash was revealed to be the gaping mouth of a cave which, though entirely natural and shaped by the elements alone, had perfectly formed granite lips drawn back in an evil grimace, and a great lolling tongue of purple stone projecting between the bared teeth, on which the giant lay sleeping with his legs and arms spread, his bound wrists and ankles shackled to a massive porphyry slab by golden manacles. Yea, you guessed it …

Prometheuz opened his eyes and groaned. Where was he? Oh yes, Mount Caucasus, where the smith of the gods, Hesiod, and his dwarves had brought him in the dead of the night, before the lame fucker, who was Prometheuz's nephew, limped back to Olympus, leaving him shackled to cold stone to start his sentence.

And as if one hundred thousand years wasn't enough, Zeus had added another punishment – but what? It was at the back of his mind, a story, or something he had been told a long, long time ago. If only Mnemosyne had been near, he could have asked her help to recover the memory. But now there was no one around save for annoying sprites of the wind ruffling his hair as dawn broke and the sun rose over a distant range of mountains.

No god is as cruel as Zeus. It was only when his Zeus smiled down on him when pronouncing judgement that at last he realized how true the ancient Olympian saying was. *No god is as cruel as Zeus*. As one, the assembled gods gasped. Mnemosyne's eyes had widened in horror, while his attorney, Dionysus, hung his head for shame. Even Poseidon, over in the Prosecution benches, was visibly shocked. All the gods assembled in Zeus's great hall knew that the sentence was a warning to each and every one of them, but only Prometheuz got to pay the price.

And now, spread-eagled (now there's a word) to a slab stone, sheltered from the worst of the elements in the mouth of a cave, Prometheuz could only follow the progress of Helios's fiery chariot, as in his god-addled mind he now thought of the sun. One moment it was dawning over the range of mountains to the east, and the next, it seemed, it was careering towards its zenith.

Looking down from the summit of the mountain where he was bi-located on the set, Jake2 didn't feel the slightest sympathy for his material double chained to a flat rock below.

What Jake had coming was payback, and entirely proportionate, in his view. He wanted him to suffer as he had, trapped in a shadow existence all these years, his only escapes when Jake slept and he took over. But even then, still he wasn't free of him – whatever Jake had been obsessing on earlier that day chasing him down the REM dreamways – the effects of alcohol being the worst come Friday nights, after Jake got drunk with his pals. Then his perceptions became clouded, and his confused state left him vulnerable to attack by the elementals which roamed the lower reaches of the dream world – iterations of the same perps now prowling the set amongst them.

All in all it had been a nightmare existence, playing second fiddle to Mr Nice Guy Jake, as he was widely perceived in the material world, but whom Jake2 knew as his cruel jailer until the day he'd been expressed from bondage by means of an AI program. Free at last, the tables were turned, he was a shadow player no longer and was in charge of the script of their twinned lives.

Half blinded by the sun, which was now dipping towards the western horizon, Prometheuz squinted up at the orange flecked sky, wondering if the speck he had just seen high above was a bird or a dust mote in his eye?

He hoped it was dust, because somehow he felt that a bird was associated with whatever he had been trying to remember, and he knew it was not a pleasant memory. For sure it was a bird up there, he realized, after trying to blink it away, but bigger. Now he could make out its great wings, as it circled closer. Was it a vulture, perhaps? No, definitely an eagle. Vultures had scrawny necks and red wattles, whereas there was nothing scrawny about this raptor, or the intent in the black eyes, as it looked down on him, the sharp point of its razor beak gleaming red from the setting sun as it swept down on him, claws extended.

'Aaaaaaaah!' he screamed, impotently, rattling his chains as the great eagle landed on his chest in a flurry of feathers, its cruel claws raking his exposed flesh, the huge wings *blotting out the setting sun,* wrapping him in shadow deeper than the blackest night.

Let there be blood. Buckets of it. Wasn't that what the perps wanted most of all? Yea, and the non-fungible entrails and real gobbets of genoplast flesh that splattered their monstrous, upturned faces as the scene ended and Zeus's eagle soared off into a non-fungible sunset.

How the perps loved it, but yet the scene was an anti-climax, as so often when what has been keenly anticipated comes around at last.

Not so for Jake2 watching from the summit of the mountain, for whom revenge was sweet, knowing that this scene with the eagle tearing at his material double's innards would be played out, over and over for the next hundred thousand years, as Zeus had ruled when he pronounced sentence on the prisoner.

INTERMISSION

Pity poor Prometheuz as the hex-v-cams pulled away, and under cover of darkness the 3D-printed mountain construction sank below the v-set, where a medic team was on standby with the best specialist equipment – heart monitors, defibrillators, IV drips, transfusion machines and supplies of O-positive blood to replace what he had lost, once they had staunched his bleeding.

'Please don't struggle, Mr Cousins,' the medic holding his head in a vice-like grip said, soothingly.

Working as a team, the other medics sutured the livid wounds on his chest and stomach - which by a miracle of genoplast tech had already begun to heal – attached an IV drip to his right arm, inserted a hose into his rectum and flushed out his colon, before swabbing him down.

'Who in heaven's name is this 'Cousins'?' the patient roared, rattling his chains that bound him to the rock. 'I keep telling you I am –'

'Hush now, lie back, please, you need to rest.'

'Gods help me,' the patient groaned, slumping back against the rock to which he was still chained. 'Give me wine, anything for the pain,' he pleaded.

'Jake ...'

Unlike the other masked faces looking down on him, this one was female, her eyes kindly and concerned.

'Jake, it's me,' the voice coach said, taking off her mask. 'Ah, I can see you recognize me now.' She smiled. 'The medics are almost finished now, and I promise you'll feel better soon.'

'Something for the pain, please,' he pleaded.

'We're not allowed to give you

anything.'

'Why?' he groaned.

'Unfortunately the contract you signed stipulated no drugs, which includes anesthetics. Nothing we can do to change that, I am sorry to say.'

'You're sorry! You're fucking sorry! How do you think I feel?' he raged.

'Jake, you are only hurting yourself,' she insisted.

'Gods, remove these chains!' he yelled, rattling them furiously.

'Sorry, but I can't help you there either, Jake.'

'You can't, really, truly?' He stared piteously up at her, tears streaming from his eyes.

'When the last Prom walked out on the set it cost FauxReel billions. *Billions,'* she repeated, emphatically. 'So I am afraid you are just going to have to get used to your golden restraints, which after all, are fur-lined. But, look on the bright side, Jake, with your marvelous new self-repairing genoplast flesh, in just a few hours you'll be ready to face anything.'

'Yea, Prom,' the medic looking on from over her shoulder tittered. 'Ready for Zeus' big bad eagle, heh heh …'

Pleased to have successfully consummated his marriage, Julian had left Carrie sleeping in her bed, downstairs in her suite of rooms.

His performance (as he thought) was altogether up to the standards he'd maintained over previous years with a succession of Pricilla sex dolls, which he always disposed of after the act (dropped into the smog from a great height being his preferred method) because then they were shop-soiled – by him. His feelings towards Carrie, he freely admitted, if only to himself, were complex. Though not a virgin, and therefore in that sense used goods, he was prepared to overlook her second-hand status in the marriage stakes, on account of the satisfaction he took from the tortures being inflicted on her ex-partner, whose progress on The Greatest Olympus Games show he was avidly following on his hand-held as he lounged in his silk dressing gown, alone (as he thought) in his cabin.

'What are you laughing at?' Carrie said, suddenly appearing at his side.

'Oh, nothing.'

'Can I see it?' she said, holding out a hand.

'Woops, it's gone.' He smiled, nervously. 'Clicked the wrong button! You'd-a thought I knew how to work them better by now. Sorry.'

'So, after we make love for the very first time, you watch porn. Is that what I now have to expect, Julius?'

'Not at all!' he waxed indignant, sitting up in his chair. 'I would never do that.'

'So what was it?'

'Well,' he sighed. 'Ok yes, in one sense, maybe it was porn, even though it was business.'

'Make up your mind, Julius,' she glowered.

'I was just vetting auditions for a new comedy live sex show we have planned for the end of the year. Sorry if I seemed to be enjoying it, but it is work, because I have to give the final say so on which actor gets picked for what role.'

*

CHAPTER 8

V-RIZON – *Serving the V-industry, since V-Genesis.*

On Saturday, 11/7/37 The global livestreaming audience of Episode 5 of FakeReel's latest adult-only blockbuster, The Greatest Olympus Games, peaked at a staggering 5.5 billion, which is 0.2 billion more than the previous record for a livestreamed show.

V-Rizon is an equal opportunities employer. Company motto: *Pursuing excellence beyond and below the horizon.* Annual t/o $(US) 64.277 trillion. V-Rizon is a division of STYX2U Corp. Inc., Registered Office, Box 346, The Hub, New Nautilus City, the Pacific Shelf. Latitude: 39.484589 Longitude: 124.90984

With a sigh, Montague-Evans looked up from the illumined holo display over on his desk, where the little icon of a radioactive turd showed the progress of the Pizza Hut.

It was presently over Pakistan, heading to its next destination.

A bottle-nosed dolphin-bot, trailing an empty pannier and returning to base for more packages, glided past the thick window glass of his office in New Nautilus, 600 fathoms below the surface of the Pacific Ocean, some 220 miles off the coast of California.

The future, Montague firmly believed, lay below the smog, not above it. Out in international waters, Governments had no jurisdiction, there were no dumb planning restrictions to get around, or petty officialdom, with their hands out for bribes. Even better, two hundred miles from the coast, no one owned the seabed, when the equivalent was not true of high altitudes, where Fatberg was building his condos for the super-rich.

Though his preparations for the next stage of his master plan to bring down FakeReal had been meticulous in every respect, Montague couldn't help worrying something might still go wrong before the outsourced covert operation started later that day.

Fatberg was such a lucky bastard. Dirt never seemed to stick to the teflon dick. He'd lost count of how many times his arch rival had over-reached himself and apparently been heading for disaster, only to come up smelling of petunias and even richer than before after his latest megalomaniac project went belly-up, losing his investors' fortunes but never a dollar of his.

Like his ridiculous 10,000 Towers to Save the World, which turned out to have increased atmospheric CO_2 rather than reversing it as had been promised. But against all the facts, such was FauxReel's control of the v-waves, what should have gone down in history as Fatberg's Folly was widely perceived to have been a noble failure, leading

Montague to speculate his hated rival had the magic algorithm of popularity up his sleeve. The news of his recent marriage, which had already gone viral on the v-waves, would do the same, unless it could be made to seem ridiculous in the eyes of the world. Hence what he had planned for FauxReel's flagship v-show in exactly 22 minutes – an intervention calculated to coincide with peak streaming figures. All totally deniable, of course ...

THE GREAT OLYMPUS GAMES –

EPISODE 24 SCENE #1

(Banner Headline Emblazoned Across The Sky)

– DAY 2: Prometheuz's Sentence –

'Only 99,999 YEARS, 364 DAYS, *and counting …'*

Groaning, Prometheuz opened his eyes. Mount Caucusus, where else? The golden light of dawn suffusing the sky, announcing day two of his sentence, had arrived. If only he could sleep out the next – what was it – yea, 99,999 YEARS 364 DAYS he had left to serve.

'Fuck you, Zeus!' he screamed, rattling his chains. 'Fuck Poseidon, fucking Hesiod, fuck Aphrodite up every orifice, and clusterfuck Dionysus Piss hole Dionysus, on Mount Olympus or wherever you are. One day, one beautiful day, I swear I will have my revenge on all of you …'

Fucking nothing, not even an echo, from the far mountaintops. He could have taken anything but this blind Olympian indifference to his fate. No god cared one jot for him …

A faint sensation of warmth seeped into his bones as, in a blaze of glory, the sun god Helios' fiery chariot crested the far ridge of mountains.

Lying on his back, manacled by his wrists and ankles to a bed of cold stone, all Prometheuz could do was scan the sky and wait for Zeus's eagle to descend and once again rip into him with its great beak and cruel claws. Overnight his belly had completely healed, and appeared smooth as a baby's bottom. From his limited perspective, flat on his back, he couldn't see so much as a mark, far less a scar of yesterday's gaping wounds to his chest and stomach – his godlike abs were like new, his self-repairing genoplast flesh totally unblemished – Yea, ripe for ruination once again. How he envied humankind their short lives and merciful death, which granted an end to pain. Not for them protracted tortures, such as he was going to have to endure for … what was it again? Prometheuz groaned once more. Yea, the next 99,999 YEARS 364 DAYS, *and counting*.

Contrary to what he thought, Prometheuz was not alone.

Always his iteration was watching— even as he wove together the storylines of Fatberg, Carrie, and now Montague Evans, into a tapestry of silken threads.

You heard it first on **the FakeBlack** TRUTHChannel.

'Question everything,
'Deny nothing …'
(Wilt Whatman)
 ID or IT? What comes first?

If you guessed, ID – wrong! No matter where they are born, whatever the culture or in which country, babies always start off as It. Isn't 'It' cuddly. 'It's' so lovely. Oh, can I hold 'it'.' That doesn't last of course. As more and more IDentity traits come to the fore, so the ITeration fades from view. Consequently, by the time the child reaches 5 years old, invariably the ITeration has completely receded into the background – and thereafter only manifests in dreams and altered mind body states.

Dawn had come and gone, noon was well past, and now, as Helios' fiery chariot dipped towards the jagged horizon, at last the moment arrived which the record 5.5 billion livestreaming the Go Games had been waiting for …

But what was this?

As Zeus' mighty eagle swooped down onto poor helpless Prometheuz, chained to his rock, three illuminated figures appeared at his side. Their sudden manifestation elicited a collective gasp from the 5.5 billion audience, the vast majority of whom instantly recognized the familiar face of Fatberg. A smaller though still significant proportion of the audience recognized the second figure to be the Pope, standing in a characteristic pose, one hand raised, clearly blessing the other two figures, facing him, heads bowed. However, only one individual out of that vast audience knew who the third figure was.

'Carrie!' Prometheuz cried, completely forgetting the pain of the eagle's great claws raking his genoplast flesh. His anguish knew no bounds, for he had realized, this was a marriage ceremony he was seeing, and it was the Pope who was pronouncing Fatberg and Carrie man and wife.

Too late, the message which flashed across the v-set, before the livestream footage was abruptly cut-off …

HACK-ATTACK-ALERT- HACK-ATTACK-ALERT …

The moment of high drama which the episode had been building towards was lost. Now all the audience (with one exception) wanted to know was the backstory of the mystery woman who had just married the most eligible bachelor in the entire world.

*

CHAPTER 9

Reuters reports: analysis of data recorded by the 152 stations of the Global Seismographic Network show the collective gasp of the estimated 5.5 billion audience of the GOGames, as they recognized the face of Fatberg, slowed the rotation of the planet by .125 of a second before it resumed its normal speed of rotation, 3.3 minutes later.

The mystery woman was soon identified as Caroline Erheart, after she was named by the former director of an obscure dance company from New Zealand which had disbanded at the start of the Emergency. However, the questions surrounding the former professional dancer only deepened.

Was she, as the host of the Saturday morning batbox show alleged, the ex-partner of the unknown actor drafted in to play Prometheuz in the FauxReel's blockbuster V-show, the GOGames? And if so, what was his connection to Fatberg, who, it was understood, had selected him over the other candidates auditioned for the role. Further investigations revealed that her supposed father, John Erheart, who had died some years before in a mountain climbing accident which was never properly explained, was in fact her guardian, and only took on the role after her Russian émigré parents and her grandmother were all murdered in their Paris apartment by unknown assailants, when she was only three years old.

Like everywhere else, speculation over these and other questions concerning Fatberg's bride was at fever pitch in Kathmandu, which was their next destination. The ancient capital of Nepal was fortunate in being situated above the prevailing smog-belt covering the Indian sub-continent, and so the emergency regulations pertaining in cities at lower altitudes, which forbid public gatherings, did not apply there.

Consequently, when the Pizza Hut landed the next morning in Durbar Square, opposite the royal palace of Hanumandhoka, a large crowd was already gathered in early morning sunshine behind metal barricades, which had been hastily erected by recently re-employed royal guards, resplendent in their new uniforms, to welcome the happy couple.

Prominent among the placards raised above the massed heads of the cheering throng, was a long banner painted with the words: *'All Nepal wishes esteemed Fatberg and his lovely bride a happy honeymoon.'*

'Does that really say what I think it does,' Carrie said, leaning over the rail of the observation deck and pointing to the banner.

'A bit over the top, isn't it,' Fatberg sniggered. 'It seems we are the talk of Kathmandu, sweetie.'

'So who let that cat out of the bag?' she said, accusingly, turning to face him. 'Our marriage was supposed to be secret.'

'I promise you I never … Oh no!' He clapped his forehead, as he suddenly realized this was all to do with the hack attack on the GO Games, which had started exactly eight hours thirty-two minutes before. 'Montague, you bastard!' he glowered.

'What are you saying?' she demanded.

'I know who's behind this. Montague-Evans. The bot king, so-called. How I hate him.'

Of course, when it comes to Fatberg, there are levels and levels. As he had correctly supposed, Montague was behind the hack attack. But though his arch-rival was also responsible for leaking what had already become known as the 'marriage tapes' to the media, in that Montague had only beaten him to the punch by a few days. Fatberg was a master of self-publicity, and despite his assurances to Carrie, he would never have passed on such an opportunity as the v-cam recording of the secret ceremony in the Vatican presented.

However, Fatberg had only planned to leak the material *after* he had concluded (successfully, he assumed), the stalled negotiations with the new Nepalese government, which was his real purpose in coming to Kathmandu, however much Carrie had always wanted to see the sights.

Over the past three years, much had changed in Kathmandu.

The city's smog-free status, which was almost unique among capital cities of the world, had attracted many wealthy new residents, who lived in the shiny high-rise developments which now ringed the old city. The exponentially increasing gap between rich and poor had fueled much resentment amongst the mostly impoverished local population.

In the two weeks since the King had been restored to power, the simmering tensions in the Old City erupted on three successive nights of rioting, which were put down with great brutality by the militarized police working in concert with armed security contractors, employed by the corporate owners of the new developments – foremost among which was the property division of FakeReal.

Clearly something had to be done, otherwise the new wealth flooding into the city would soon go elsewhere, but what, exactly? Only Fatberg had the answer, as ever. But his price for furnishing the solution was high. Very, very high.

*

THE GREAT OLYMPUS GAMES - EPISODE 25

(Banner Headline Emblazoned Across The Sky)

– DAY 3: Prometheuz's Sentence –

'Only 99,999 YEARS, 363 DAYS *and counting!'*

'Not good, not good,' the CEO of Styx2U, Montague Evans, mumbled to himself, oblivious to the leatherback turtle (which were thought to be extinct), nosing past the thick glass of his office window some 600 fathoms below the surface of the Pacific Ocean. He was scanning the threads on the chat-boxes following the latest GOGames show, which he had livestreamed in his V-room only an hour before.

Instead of the audience figures plummeting after the plug was pulled on the previous episode, as he had confidently anticipated, this time they were actually up at an incredible 5.7 billion, which was a new world record for any livestreamed show. Worse still, support was now building across all sectors for the dud actor in the main role (drafted in after Montague had bribed the previous one to walk out) over his anguished reaction to the second hack attack, in which the mystery woman had been named as Carrie Erheart and revealed to be his ex-partner.

Once again, against all expectations, Fatberg had benefited, when by now his reputation should have been well into negative territory. Instead, it was up again on Trustpilot, at an unbelievable 7.9, way above any other CEO, and three clear points ahead of his own trust rating. It seemed there was no way to make mud stick to the teflon dick, he considered ruefully, as he clicked onto the next feed.

'What the ..? Montague gasped, staring goggle-eyed at the thread that jumped out at him from the screen of his handheld. 'Of all the lucky bastards ... No! No! No!' he protested loudly, to a deity he didn't believe in, 'Please God don't let this be true!'

*

Carrie was out shopping when the news got through to the palace.

His Royal Highness, King Girvanyuddha Bikrama Shah II, was even more impressed after the Russian ambassador's phone call was finally answered. The loud ringing had continued for two minutes 45 seconds according to Fatberg's calculations, until a royal equerry who was in attendance managed to locate the antiquated bakelite telephone, which hadn't rung for several years, under some bejeweled cushions.

'It's for you!' the King said, after answering and exchanging pleasantries with the ambassador, a new note to his Highness' baritone voice suggesting he was feeling a little upstaged as he held out the handset to Fatberg.

'Yes, I am … Yes, you are speaking to me, Mr Ambassador. No, no, she's out presently … What …? No, no. Shopping. You know, women … Ha ha … What did you say..? Yes, the world over … I am sure she … um her Royal Highness will be delighted to accept the invitation. Saint Basil's you say. The President insists. Uh huh. Protocol, yes. I'll instruct my appointments manager to get back to you, to make necessary arrangements once I, ah, have, um, discussed things with her ... Yes, indeed, delighted. The pleasure is mutual ... Please pass on my regards to your esteemed President. Thank you again ... Goodbye.'

Looking back on his audience with the King, Fatberg realized it was the phone call that clinched the deal.

Carrie being who she now was had elevated him in the eyes of the King to her royal consort, the consort of the Tsarina of all Russia in all but name, prior to her coronation in Saint Basil's cathedral in Moscow.

He was the owner of the highest mountain of all, (which the Nepalese called Sagarmatha, meaning "the Head of the Earth touching the Heaven.") and soon to be renamed The Fatberg, on GPS and the next editions of the atlases of the world, once the details of the compensation package with the Nepalese government were finalized. A few ticks and dots were all that was remained to complete after the King and he shook on deal. He was on top of the world. What could go wrong now?

*

It started out as a spontaneous demonstration by a few neighbors, leaning out of the unsealed and open windows of their apartments, chanting 'Free Prom! Free Prom! The chanting quickly spread, until it rang out in streets around the city, and then across the whole world. At last the pent-up rage, engendered by three years of the universal shut-in, had found expression, not just in the support for Prometheuz, who had become emblematic for the plight of the great majority, but the hatred people everywhere had for their corporate captors, who had trashed the world and robbed them of so much. And center stage, head and shoulders above the rest, who else but Fatberg, now firmly in the frame as the chief culprit to blame ...

The story continues, in 3rd book of the XREAL Series, which will be released later in 2022.

INKISTAN
.COM

Will Lorimer is the author of 14 novels, find them on Inkistan.com

Discover Will's Art on willlorimer.com